JOSEPH
AND
THE
OLD
MAN

STONEWALL INN EDITIONS

Michael Denneny, General Editor

Buddies by Ethan Mordden
Joseph and The Old Man by Christopher Davis
Blackbird by Larry Duplechan
Gay Priest by Malcolm Boyd

JOSEPH AND THE OLD MAN

by
Christopher Davis

ST. MARTIN'S PRESS
New York

Design by Manny Paul

Library of Congress Cataloging-in-Publication Data

Davis, Chris.
    Joseph and the old man.

    I. Title.
PS3554.A9329J67   1986   813'.54   86-3666
ISBN 0-312-44489-3
ISBN 0-312-01052-4 (Pbk.)

First Edition

10 9 8 7 6 5 4 3 2 1

This book is for Michael O.
and for Marcia.

The author acknowledges, with gratitude,
the invaluable advice of his editor, Michael Denneny.

JOSEPH
AND
THE
OLD
MAN

The two of them, the old man and the young man, were working together in a room that looked out on the sea. The old man wrote books about men and women who existed only in his imagination; he wrote of love, of sadness; sometimes he wrote movingly about death but he preferred to write about life. While he wrote he faced the sea and he heard the sound of the waves through the open glass doors, and occasionally he lifted his head and looked across his desk and out toward the water and then sometimes he would put down his pen and take off the glasses he used when he worked and let his eyes drift out of focus until he saw only a moving blur and he would think of the young man in the room and sometimes, too, he would remember his own youth. The young man faced a white wall; his back was toward the sea. He wrote with a typewriter. He wrote of wars and nations and political theories and he wrote of men who had changed history and of the deaths that had resulted.

The two of them, the old man and the young man—his name was Joe—worked on through the morning quietly but accompanied by the sound of the sea, by the voices and laughter of the people on the beach, and by the sound of Joe's typewriter. They worked until it was past noon and gradually the old man became aware that the typewriter was silent and he put down his pen and turned back toward Joe. Joe had turned his chair around and was leaning back with his hands behind his head, facing the sea.

1

"Looks like a good beach day," he said.

"That it does," the old man replied, "that it does."

Then, as they did almost every day it did not rain, they went to the beach. Joe was young and trim and his friend—his name was Oswald but Joe always called him Old Man, with affection—was not young but still trim. Joe wore his hair, brown but reddened by the sun, long, on his shoulders, and at Joe's asking the old man did too. The old man's hair was thick and white and when he walked in the wind with his young friend their hair, white and red-brown, blew about their faces and the attention of curious newcomers to the island was often attracted.

"Who are they?" the curious would ask if they did not recognize the old man from his photographs, and then they would be told names and facts. Then they would sometimes say, "The old man must pay him," or if they did not say it they often thought it, and whether they said it or thought it they were wrong.

That day, however, there was no wind to blow their hair and there were no newcomers to be curious and when the old man and Joe went out to the beach they spoke kindly and familiarly to the people they saw and the people they saw spoke kindly and familiarly in return. It was an intensely bright day. Sunlight danced on the waves and broke into showers of brilliant fragments as the waves swelled, crested, and collapsed into roiling foam. The dunes extended as far as they could see and were laced with snow fence and spotted with beach grass. In the distance the sand seemed to move in the bright light, and the horizon faded into an opalescent haze.

"How'd it go, Old Man?" Joe asked when they were settled on the beach and after they had spoken to the people near them. Joe and the old man never discussed work while they were doing it or before they started, but only after they had both finished for the day.

"Not too bad today. Better than yesterday."

2

"That's good."

"I never used to think that thinking could be so exhausting, but it is," the old man said. "This may be my last book," he said after a pause.

"Oh come on," Joe said. "You know that as soon as this one is finished you'll have the itch to go on to something else. Besides, you shouldn't tempt the gods."

"Tempt the gods." The old man laughed. "Is that my young atheistic friend talking about tempting the gods?"

"I said gods, not God."

"Which ones did you have in mind?"

Someone near them threw a piece of a sandwich out onto the sand and the air was suddenly filled with screeching gulls. They scrambled for the pieces of food and then looked for more. Joe threw a shell at them and they moved a little away and stood watching.

"To them, you're probably a god," the old man said. "You can provide manna and have the power of destruction."

"Yes, but I can't fly."

"Do you remember Philip of Macedon?" Joe asked, a minute or two later.

"I'm old," the old man said, "but not that old. What about him?"

"He tempted the gods. On the day after his daughter's wedding he ordered a great festival, with a procession in honor of the gods followed by athletic games. Statues of the twelve gods of Olympus were carried in the procession and Philip added a statue of himself to those of the gods."

"He must have been a very confident man," the old man said.

"Maybe. It didn't help though. He was stabbed and killed as he entered the arena where the games were to be held."

"I don't think that saying this might be my last book is tempting fate in quite the same way as forcing my inclusion in the ranks of the immortals."

3

"No, maybe not. But I still don't like to hear you say it."

They lay quietly for a while and their skin was hot under the sun and sweat began to bead on their foreheads and run down the sides of their faces. Joe lay on his back with his eyes closed and the old man lay flat on his back and looked up at the blue sky but away from the sun.

"You know," the old man said, "maybe they took him."

"What?"

"The gods. Maybe they took Philip. He couldn't be a god and walk around on earth like an ordinary mortal could he? Maybe the gods accepted him into their midst and there was no more need for his body."

"That's certainly a different way of looking at it: Philip was being rewarded, not punished."

"That's why I write fiction and you write those dull papers and articles."

Joe was silent for a minute, thinking.

"Alexander," he said. "Philip's son." He turned toward the old man. "You know, Alexander the Great."

"I've heard the name," the old man said dryly. "You've only been writing about him all summer."

Joe went on: "Alexander deified himself too, and a year or so later he was dead. Perhaps the gods spent the year deciding if they should take him."

"If so, his father probably argued against him."

"Maybe," Joe said. "We all know how Alexander turned out. Freud might have said it was because his father rejected him when he was alive and, if that was true, maybe the rejection continued when his father became a god."

"You know," the old man said, "you too could write fiction."

Joe smiled, and he sat up and looked out at the sea. "I wonder how Alexander felt when he stood on the shore of the Indian Ocean and knew that he had conquered most of the world," he said.

The old man did not answer. He also sat up and looked out at the sea.

"You know, Old Man," Joe went on, "if I were Alexander I'd be dead in three years. And already I would have accomplished more than any other man in history."

"Alexander was an immature, bloodthirsty maniac," the old man said.

"Yes. Well, maybe. But that didn't matter. Look what he accomplished. He spread Greek civilization through much of the world of his time. He advanced the course of history."

"Yes, but at what cost?"

Joe turned to look at the old man. "That just doesn't matter."

"Yes it does matter." The old man raised his voice and people near them looked over, but he ignored them and continued:

"I know history too. You wonder how he felt on the shores of the Indian Ocean after his swing through India. I wonder how he felt on the shores of the Mediterranean after the sack of Tyre, where he had the men killed and the women and children enslaved. He had two thousand men crucified along the beach, you know. Can you imagine those days? I've stood on that beach. It's beautiful. Can you imagine it thick with crosses? Can you imagine the cries and the screams and the pleas to the gods for deliverance? The sobbing of tortured men? And then later the stench? The gulls must have fed on the bodies as they rotted in the sun."

The old man was agitated now.

"No, my friend, it doesn't matter," Joe said. "Two thousand men, two million men, are insignificant in the progress of history."

The old man knew that it was an argument without resolution and he sighed. He relaxed a little.

"You need some of the compassion of the man whose name you carry," he said.

5

"Who, Joseph? The one who was sold as a slave and then sucked up to his masters until he became powerful and wealthy? If he had been a little more ambitious he might have been able to do what Alexander did: conquer Egypt."

"No, not that Joseph. Joseph the husband of Mary."

"What did he do that was so compassionate?"

"When he found Mary pregnant he didn't abandon her to the punishment of Hebraic law. The law says that if a man marries a woman he finds not to be a virgin she is to be taken to the door of her father's house and stoned to death."

"He may have had a personal knowledge of how she came to be pregnant," Joe said, and he laughed.

"You should be more like Joseph," the old man insisted. "You're always writing about wars and conquests. If everyone were like you the world would be at war. Everyone would be trying to get history to march to their song. If everyone were like Joseph—forgiving, compassionate—there would always be peace."

"Now, Old Man, I'm going to tell you something about someone else who was named Oswald, Oswald Spengler. He wrote that life doesn't allow the choice between war and peace but only the choice between victory and ruin, and he also wrote that there could only be peace as long as the vast majority of people were willing to be subjugated by others who did not renounce war and were more powerful."

"You know the trouble with what you write about?" the old man said. "You start to believe it."

"A little," Joe said. "But it's not as important to me as this." He waved toward the beach, and the old man agreed with him.

They were quiet again, and they lay back and looked at the sky. The two of them often had long discussions on a vast range of topics. They talked about art, music, literature, history, politics, psychology, linguistics, philosophy, physics, and more, and as the range of topics expanded their library did

6

also. They enjoyed their conversations and they learned from their conversations and from each other. The young man learned many things about life from the old man and he learned how ideas from different intellectual disciplines fit together; the old man learned from the young man about the young, who were different than he had been when he had been young, and when he learned about the young he learned about how the world was and how it might be in the future, which was different than the way he felt it and remembered it, and both the young and the old man always learned about each other.

They were uncomfortable in the heat of the sun, the old man more so than the young, and they wiped their faces with a small towel.

"How about a dip, Old Man?" Joe asked.

"That would be fine, just fine," the old man said, and they stood up and walked to the water.

They dove through the breaking waves. The old man was slower than the young man, but he followed and when they were past the point where the waves were breaking they bobbed up and down with the swells.

"I'm going to swim," Joe said. "You coming?"

"I'm still breathing, aren't I?" the old man answered, and they started to swim down the island parallel to the beach. The old man had once been a powerful swimmer, but he was no longer. However, he swam steadily with clean, practiced strokes that barely splashed in the water, and the young man swam beside him. The young man swam easily beside the old man and he did not hurry him. They swam until the old man began to breathe hard and his arms began to make a splash when they entered the water.

"Come on, Old Man, you've had enough," Joe said.

"Who are you, my mother?" the old man answered, but he turned toward shore.

They had come several hundred yards down the beach

7

and were in a section of the island that was a national park and where there were no houses. They were alone on the beach and they sat on the fine dry sand above the swash at the high tide line and dried in the sun. When they were dry, and the old man had rested awhile, they started walking down the beach in the direction in which they had been swimming. The sand was hot under their feet so they turned down and walked just above the water, and if a wave was pushed unexpectedly high on the beach they did not move to avoid it but let the water run over their feet. A sandpiper rushed away in front of them, following the swash and occasionally stopping to pick at something before rushing on. Joe picked up a starfish that had been washed up on the sand and threw it back into the water.

"Oh, so you do have some compassion," the old man said.

Joe smiled. "Let's walk through the woods," he said, pointing to some steps that led over the dunes to a boardwalk that ambled down into a hollow behind the dunes and then over a hill and down into a forest dense with holly, red maple, blackgum, and sassafras. They turned toward the steps and as they crossed the upper beach the old man pointed out clumps of seaside spurge, sea rocket, and seabeach sandwort growing on the foredunes. They climbed the steps and turned back to look at the ocean. The waves threw up tiny droplets of water that evaporated in the hot sun before they fell, leaving microscopic salt crystals hanging in the air that were then blown inland in a fine haze by the onshore breeze. They walked down behind the dunes and pulled some leaves from a bayberry bush, crushed them in their hands, and held their hands to their faces and inhaled the greensmell of the bayberry as they climbed the hill before descending into the forest.

They were on Fire Island, part of a barrier beach extending along the south shore of Long Island. Most of the vegetation on the island was stunted by the sea spray. However, there the trees were protected by unusually high dunes and

8

they had, over the decades, grown into a dense, moist forest. The boardwalk was shaded and cool, and as they walked on it they tried to identify all of the plants and trees they saw. Poison ivy and impenetrable bull brier were everywhere so they did not leave the walk but followed it as it twisted and climbed and dipped through the woods. They did not talk about much except plants.

In two places the boardwalk broadened into a square deck where there were benches to sit on and enjoy the woods and the calling of the birds. In one of the deck areas they found a dead herring gull that had obviously died in a struggle with an animal, probably a dog. Feathers were scattered on the deck and out under the trees, and the bird's breast had been eaten away.

The old man looked at the gull. "Can you imagine its final moments?" he said. "It must have known as much terror as a bird can know. It must have screamed and cried and tried to escape. And then it died in fiery pain."

"Poor thing," Joe said.

"Now try to imagine the death of just one of those two thousand men your great Alexander crucified on the beach that bloody day after he conquered Tyre. Did the man have a family? A son he saw slashed in the stomach with a sword? A wife or a daughter he saw raped by a line of brutal men? Can you imagine the pain of his arms being slowly pulled out of their sockets? His thirst?" The old man was becoming agitated again. "And you say that doesn't matter?"

Joe sighed. He did not like to argue with the old man, but he was young and could not be silent.

"Yes, Old Man, the death of one man does matter. But it is also a fact that without wars and death history would have been different in ways we can't imagine. Those wars got us where we are, and war will probably continue to shape history."

"You know," the old man said, "with people like you

9

thinking about and planning war there's sure to be another one."

"But if we don't plan, others—the Russians, the Chinese—will."

"What if neither side did?"

"Now you know, and I know, that we wouldn't if we could be sure that no one else would, but how would we know that no one else was planning? It's human nature to try to gain the advantage and it's human nature not to really trust someone you don't know. Hell, it's the nature of life to be destructive. Look at that poor gull."

"That gull was killed for food, not for wanton bloodlust."

"How do you know? Don't you think that the dog, or whatever killed it, enjoyed the chase and the kill?"

"Maybe, but I still feel sorry for the gull and I think that whenever you write about war you should always try to visualize the death of just one man or woman, or boy or girl, who died, or who will die, in the war you're writing about, and I think that you should hold that image as long as you write whatever you're writing."

While they talked they leaned against the rail that surrounded the deck and now Joe noticed that the old man still seemed tired from the swim and the walk in the sand.

"Let's sit for a while," he said, and they went to a bench. They sat in a small patch of sunlight that had pierced through the covering of branches and leaves overhead and their hair shined in the sunlight.

"Do you think there will ever be a nuclear war?" the old man asked.

"Yes, I do," Joe said, "and it will probably destroy much of the earth. But a new civilization will grow from the ruins and a new epoch of history will begin."

The old man looked sad, and still a little tired.

10

"You know," Joe said, very gently, "I think you're afraid of death."

"Not death. Dying. It's the path that leads up to that instant that worries me, not the instant itself, or after."

"Me too. I hope I die in my sleep. No pain. No terror."

"I don't think I want that," the old man said. "I want to know what's happening; I just want it to be gentle and easy. As you said, no pain."

"My son, you will probably outlive me, the way you're going," Joe said. He put his arm across the old man's shoulders.

"Maybe," the old man replied.

They sat quietly, looking into the sun-spotted forest. Neither of them believed that the old man would live longer, but they pretended that they did and they no longer spoke of wars or great men. Finally the old man stood up, after five or ten minutes had passed.

"Come on, my young friend," he said. "We left our things on the beach more than an hour ago."

"No one will take them," Joe said, but he got up too and together they followed the boardwalk back to the beach, and again the old man pointed out the sea rocket with its delicate pale lavender blossoms.

They again walked in the cool sand below the high tide line and let the water wash over their feet. They listened to the sound of the pebbles and fragments of shells caught in the roil of the waves, a sound like that of thousands of tiny bamboo wind chimes blowing gently in the wind. The old man pointed to the track made by one of the police dune bikes that had gone down the beach while they had been in the forest. Joe threw more starfish back into the ocean, but there were so many on the beach that he soon stopped and after that he walked around them or stepped over them. The waves had also thrown jellyfish up on the sand and the gelatinous, trans-

11

parent smears could be seen glistening in the sun as the old man and the young man walked down the beach.

In front of them a gull dove into the water and came out with a crab, which it dropped on the sand. The old man held Joe back and they watched as the crab tried to crawl away, surrounded by pursuing gulls. One of the birds caught the crab, turned it on its back deftly, and killed it by piercing the crab's shell with its beak. The gull ripped off a claw and flew away, and the carcass was fallen upon by the gull's companions.

"That's how life goes on," Joe said.

"Yes," the old man answered, "but I like to think that we're a little better than the gulls and the crabs."

Joe laughed. "I'm not so sure," he said.

They walked on. "Are you sure you don't want to go into the city with me tomorrow?" Joe asked.

"I'm sure," the old man said. "You'll be busy all day and there's nothing I want to do there. Besides, it's supposed to be hot tomorrow."

"Suit yourself," Joe said.

"When are you leaving?"

"Early. I told Ann I'd be in by ten so I should catch a ferry that leaves around seven."

"I don't know how you managed it," the old man said. "In all the years I taught I never had a secretary who wasn't either illiterate, incompetent, or sick all the time. And you get a sainted female Shakespeare who never has as much as a cold."

"It's my smile." Joe smiled.

"How long do you think you'll be?"

"I don't know. I want to get everything set up for the fall semester. It's less than a month away, you know."

"I know," the old man said. "I still miss it a little. The students coming back and all."

"You've got me," Joe said, and they both smiled.

They walked on and soon they were in front of the first house in Cherry Grove, and they passed a house where an Israeli and an American flag snapped in the wind, and down the beach they could see their towels. They walked on, enjoying the sun, and when they reached their towels Joe went swimming again, but the old man was tired and he sat on the beach and watched.

Joe was tanned and lean and sleek and his hair was slicked back by the water and he swam and dove with unselfconscious ease. The old man was sad because he was no longer young and no longer sleek and Joe was, but then, watching the young man playing in the water, he thought of otters and he laughed. He laughed at himself and he laughed at the thought of otters and he was no longer sad. He then lay back in the sun and closed his eyes and passed in and out of sleep, lulled by the sound of the waves.

Joe continued to swim, and while he swam a friend of his and the old man's who was young and a powerful swimmer like Joe swam out to meet him and together they swam straight out to sea until the people on the beach looked small and distant, and then they turned and pushed slowly toward shore, rising and falling with the waves.

"How's the old man?" Joe's friend asked. Friends of Joe and the old man had become accustomed to Joe calling the old man Old Man and they grew into the habit of doing it also. It was used casually and affectionately and neither the old man nor Joe minded, although occasionally the old man would have a guest who would be discomfited to hear young men call out "Hello, Old Man" or say "How are you, Old Man" when the old man and his guest were out walking.

"He's fine," Joe said. "I worry about him sometimes, but he's fine."

"So what makes you worry?" his friend asked as they continued to rise and fall with the waves.

"Oh, he daydreams some now, and sometimes he rambles

13

a little, and occasionally he forgets what he's talking about. But he's pretty healthy, so I guess I shouldn't worry too much."

"I saw you two swimming earlier, and he still swims OK for an old guy. Hell, he swims OK for a young guy."

"That he does," Joe said, "and he still writes as well as he ever did."

"I'm glad," his friend said, and he dove down into the water and emerged some distance away. He waited for Joe to catch up.

"Looks like he's sleeping," he said.

"He was a little tired," Joe replied, and they swam through the breakers and ran up on the beach. The old man was asleep. Joe took his towel and sat a little distance away with his friend, watching the old man and talking quietly.

Soon the old man awoke. He had been dreaming about swimming in a fine tropical sea off a gleaming white sand beach and the sound of the waves breaking on the Fire Island shore had become the sound of his arms entering the water again and again and again, steadily. In the first instants of wakefulness he was disoriented and he wondered why he was not in the water when he could still hear himself swimming, but his mind cleared quickly and he sat up. Joe and his friend came over.

"Hello Carl," the old man said. "Did I sleep long?" he asked Joe.

"Not long," Joe said. "Maybe thirty minutes. It's good for you."

"Yes mother," the old man said. Carl laughed.

"It must be near four," Joe said, and the old man said, "Must be," and he stood up and they began to collect their things.

"Will we see you later this afternoon, Carl?" the old man asked.

"I think so. I'm going to bring a friend if that's OK," Carl said. "I met him yesterday on the beach."

"You know it is," Joe said, and then he and the old man turned toward their house.

"See you later," he called to his friend, and the old man waved and Carl waved back.

"See you later," Carl called, and he walked down the beach toward the east, in the direction of the Pines.

The old man was a well-known writer. He had won the Pulitzer twice, and whenever he published a new book it was featured on the front page of *The New York Times Book Review* and was reviewed throughout the country. He had once been a solitary, private, shy man who seldom had visitors, but Joe had changed that. In his first summer on the island with the old man Joe had been a very young man and he had made many friends and his friends often came to visit without invitations as everyone there does, and then his friends met the old man, who was a younger old man then but still not a young man, and word that the old man was on the island spread, and they had many, many visitors. The old man had not complained because he liked Joe and he realized that Joe was young, but at the end of the summer Joe discovered that the old man had not written very much and that what he had written was not very good.

The first day of the following summer that they were on the island many of their friends from the previous summer came to the house to say hello, and when they came Joe thanked them for coming and did not ask them in but asked them to return at five in the afternoon for a glass of wine. When five o'clock came, people came, and Joe asked them in and gave everyone who wanted one a glass of wine, and they all talked and laughed. Gradually, as the glasses emptied, people became aware that no more wine was being offered. At

15

first they were confused, but then they began to understand and when they began to understand they began to say good-bye, and everyone was gone by six-thirty.

All through that summer Joe did the same, and sometimes when there were many people already there and someone else came to the door Joe would thank them for coming but ask them to come back on another day. Through the years that Joe and the old man had come to the island, ten now, their after-noon gatherings had become endowed by custom with a set of rules: If you drank anything you drank what was offered, and everyone drank the same thing—usually wine, but sometimes the old man made daiquiris or mimosas; you seldom were given more than two glasses of whatever it was and you did not ask for more; you never arrived before five and you left by six-thirty unless you were asked to join Joe and the old man for dinner, which happened rarely, and you usually took a walk down the beach in front of the house to look at the deck and through the glass doors to see how many people were there, and if it looked like there were more than a handful you came back another day; you only went on Wednesday or Sat-urday, and you did not go if one of them was away.

Both Joe and the old man enjoyed their Afternoons. Sometimes the guests were other writers who lived on the is-land in the summer; sometimes they were the young or the curious, or both, who wanted to meet the old man; some-times, and these were the only people who came more than once a week, they were young friends of Joe's. Everyone who came enjoyed themselves, and they often learned too because Joe and the old man would lead the conversation into areas that interested them. People did not often talk about living politicians, but the history of religion was a frequent topic.

When Joe and the old man reached the top of the steps that led over the dunes to their house they stopped and looked back at the sea.

"Look at those waves," Joe said. "They're the highest they've been this summer."

"It's that hurricane out in the Atlantic somewhere," the old man told him.

"I know," Joe said, "but it's a long way out. There aren't even any clouds here."

The old man and the young man looked at the sea and the sky for a little longer then turned toward the house.

"Looks like the tide will really be high this evening," the old man said as they turned away. "We'll have to watch it."

They brushed off their feet outside the house and went in a door on the side away from the sea and came into the kitchen. They put their towels on a chair.

"I'm going for the mail," the old man said. "Coming?"

"Your fans will be here in an hour or so," Joe said. "You'd better shower."

"There's plenty of time."

Joe shook his head. "Why don't you go and I'll stay here and shower and get something ready. You wouldn't want to disappoint your admirers."

"My admirers, hell. In this place beauty comes before age," the old man said.

They both smiled, and they both knew that what the old man had said was generally true, but they both knew also that many people came to see the old man, and that made the old man happy and Joe happy too.

"You'd better hurry up," Joe said.

"I'm going, I'm going." The old man took a shirt from a closet near the door and put it on. "Do we need anything from the store?" he asked, although he did not usually shop for them.

"Are we eating in or out?"

"You're not going to be here tomorrow. Let's eat out."

"That would be nice," Joe said. "Then we don't need anything."

17

The old man went for the mail and Joe showered and dressed and was hanging out the towels when the old man returned. The house was surrounded by a wooden deck and the deck was enclosed on the sides by a wooden fence. On the side of the deck facing the sea the fence became a low rail, and on the side closest to the walk the fence had a gate in it. Joe was hanging the towels over the fence when the old man came through the gate. The old man rang the bell that hung on a post by the gate as he came in.

"Anything for me?" Joe asked.

"You got a letter," the old man said. "I didn't get a damned thing, so I bought a paper. Maybe everybody's forgotten me."

The old man liked to receive mail, and when he received a letter from anyone except Joe he read it carefully and then put it in his desk. The next day he read it again and then carefully, methodically, ripped it into tiny squares and discarded it. Letters from Joe he kept in a safe deposit box in a bank in Manhattan and once or twice a year he went to the bank and sat in a little room with the box of Joe's letters in front of him and read them all. If there were people in the other little rooms they would hear him chuckle or sometimes laugh loudly, and then sometimes after he had been heard laughing, and when he was finished with the letters and had left the room to carry the box back to the vault, someone who had heard him laughing would recognize him from his photographs and would wonder what he had been laughing about or if he was completely sane.

Today, however, there were no letters from anyone else and Joe was with him.

"I haven't forgotten you," Joe said as he held the door open for the old man, "and you'd better get into the shower."

"I know, I know," said the old man, and he went to put the paper on his desk and then to shower.

The shower was across from the kitchen and as Joe

worked in the kitchen he heard the old man begin to sing. The old man always sang in the shower. In the morning he often half sang and half hummed a wandering, tuneless song that rose and fell as he raised or lowered an arm or as the water became hotter or colder. It had been a good day for the old man and this afternoon he sang real songs. He did not sing any of them all of the way though but strung together fragments of several. Joe smiled as the old man sang out "Oh what a beautiful MORN-ing, oh-what-a-beau-ti-ful-day, da da da da da da Daaaa da, da-da-da-da-da-da-da," and then went into "Sunrise, Sunset." After that there was a minute or two of quiet and then Joe heard the seguidilla from *Carmen* and he laughed aloud. The old man sang through a medley of bits and pieces of arias and choruses from *Carmen* and then the water stopped.

"That was some concert," Joe said when the bathroom door opened.

The old man grinned and went into the front room and up to the loft to dress. Joe went into the front room and put on a recording of *Carmen* and the old man sang out with the overture, and always there was the sound of the sea.

Carl arrived first, with his friend, and when he did he rang the bell by the gate and walked through the gate and across the deck that surrounded the house and up to the door that led into the kitchen. Joe went to the door when he heard the bell.

"Come in," he said to Carl and his friend.

"Hi, I'm Joe," he said to Carl's friend.

"This is Lonny," Carl told him, and Lonny said hello.

Lonny was very thin and his hair was very blond, although where his hair parted it looked dark close to his head. He smiled widely.

Joe handed Carl and his friend glasses of wine. "Company," he called to the old man.

"It's champagne!" Lonny said.

19

"Is it all right?" Joe asked. The glass he had filled for himself was still on the table and now he picked it up and took a sip.

Carl answered: "I'll say. High-school teachers who have to tend bar in the summer to afford to live out here are accustomed to beer."

"It's good," his friend said, and the old man came into the room.

"Hi. I'm the old man," he said to Lonny.

"I'm Lonny," Lonny said. "What should I call you?" he asked, not certain if the old man was making fun of him in some way he did not understand.

"Just call me Old Man," the old man said. "Everyone else does."

"Come on in," Joe said, and he picked up the plate of cold vegetables he had prepared and went into the large room that faced the sea, followed by the others.

"Inside or outside?" he asked.

"Let's go out," the old man said. Joe turned off the stereo and they went out on the part of the deck that faced the sea. Although there were two lounge chairs leaning, folded, against the side of the house, they sat in smaller chairs with canvas seats and canvas backs. Joe put the plate of vegetables on a low, round table. They did not sit around the table but sat in a semicircle open toward the sea.

"Where are you from?" the old man asked Lonny.

"All over," Lonny said. "I worked the East Coast last winter and spring and this fall I'll be in New York."

"You worked the East Coast?"

"I'm an erotic dancer."

"That's nice," the old man said. He was amused, but he meant that it was nice and he and Lonny talked about dancing and about what makes dancing erotic and through the old man's questions and observations Lonny articulated ideas he did not know he had.

20

Joe and Carl listened to the old man and Lonny, and Joe smiled. They heard a woman's voice from inside.

"Hey. This is Wednesday, isn't it?" someone called, and Joe went into the house and the others stood up. When Joe came back he had two women with him and he was carrying a bottle of champagne and two glasses.

"Hello Elizabeth," the old man said to one of the women, a thin, gray-haired woman wearing tan slacks and a white blouse. "We haven't seen you in more than a month."

"Hello yourself," the woman said. She held out her cheek to be kissed.

"Hello Mildred," the old man said to Elizabeth's companion, and then everyone said hello. Joe brought two more chairs and now everyone except Mildred sat in a semicircle around the table.

Mildred had a red complexion and puffy face and had, over the years, been asked to leave most of the bars on the island at least once, and she had been banned permanently from a few. She wore a billowy print dress and smelled faintly boozy, and she sat in a chair holding her glass and she looked dourly out to sea.

"How have you been?" the old man asked her, and she did not have much good to say about the weather or about the new people on the island that summer or about the daytrippers she could see on the beach. Then she told him that the boy on the water taxi they had taken down the island had been rude to her and had told her to sit down.

Throughout it all the old man listened pleasantly and understandingly, and suddenly the woman was through and again she sat and looked dourly out to sea.

The others had been talking among themselves, and now the old man turned to Elizabeth.

"How is the psychiatry business?" he asked.

"Not very busy," Elizabeth said. "I only keep a few

21

patients now, and I don't see them regularly during the summer."

The old man nodded, and she went on:

"I've been re-reading your books this summer. They're not bad." She smiled at the old man as though they shared a secret.

"God," he said. "I wish I could burn some of them now. Especially that sappy thing I wrote when I was young and thought I was in love."

"You mean *Magnificent Madness*?"

"That's the one," the old man said. "I think it's embarrassing. I can't read it now."

"I think Oswald is right," Mildred said, without turning from the sea. "It is embarrassing to read."

"Now don't be mean," Elizabeth said.

"What are you working on now?" she asked the old man.

The old man looked across the table at Joe, who was partially turned away and talking to Lonny and Carl. "It's a novel about a young man," he said quietly. "I don't know if I'll ever publish it because it's so personal, but I want Joe to have it."

"Does he know what you're writing?"

"Not really. He never reads much of my work before it's finished because he says he doesn't want to influence me. But he has read a little of it."

"What's Joe working on?" Elizabeth asked, and as the old man started to answer they heard the bell that hung by the gate on the other side of the house. The old man stopped and looked at Joe.

"Come on, Lonny," Joe said. "Let's see who it is. You can help me with the champagne."

The bell rang again.

Lonny and Joe did not go through the house but walked around the side on the deck. The front gate was open and a late-middle-aged man and woman were outside. The man was wearing a light-colored sports jacket and the woman was wearing a tailored dress and carrying a purse. They looked out of place on the island on a hot August afternoon.

"Hello," Joe said.

The couple looked at Joe, who was shirtless, and at Lonny, who grinned, and then they looked at each other. The man nervously started into a speech that sounded rehearsed.

"Does Oswald Stevenson live here?" he asked.

"Yes," Joe said. "Come in."

The man did not come in, but continued:

"Well, I teach English in high school in Moira—"

"That's in northern New York," his wife said.

"—and I've always wanted to meet Mr. Stevenson so I wrote to his publisher who sent me the address of Mr. Stevenson's agent, Mr. Nolan, and I wrote to him and he wrote back that I, we, could come out here on a Wednesday afternoon at five o'clock. I tried to call ahead but I couldn't get a number."

"We don't have a telephone out here," Joe said, "but come in." He led the man and woman and Lonny into the kitchen and gave the man and woman each a glass.

"Could you bring a bottle of champagne from the refrigerator," he said to Lonny, and he led the couple into the front room.

"Everyone's out on the deck," Joe said.

The man stopped inside and looked around the room. It was a large light-filled room that occupied most of the space in the house. Across one end was a loft for sleeping, and the room itself was pleasantly but sparsely furnished. Under the loft were two rooms: the bathroom, and a room that they used as a library and guest room.

The man walked over to Joe's desk.

"Is this where he writes?"

"No," Joe said. "That's where I work. He works there." He pointed to the old man's desk.

Lonny had the champagne open, and he came in and filled the couple's glasses. The woman stared at him.

23

"Are you a writer?" the man asked Joe.

"No, I teach history."

Lonny went past them out onto the deck. "Let's go out," Joe said. "Could you get that chair?" he asked the man and indicated another canvas chair folded against the wall. The man handed his glass to his wife and picked up the chair.

"What's your name?" Joe asked as they stepped onto the deck.

"Drew. Michael Drew," the man said. "And this is Paula."

Everyone on the deck, except Mildred, stood up when they came out.

"This is Mr. and Mrs. Drew," Joe said to the old man. "They came down from upstate to see you."

The old man stepped forward, and Mr. Drew spoke.

"I teach English in high school in Moira, in—"

"That's in northern New York," his wife said.

"—and I've always wanted to meet you, so I wrote to your publisher and he sent me the name of your agent, and I wrote to your agent and he said that I—"

"We," said Mrs. Drew.

"—we, could come out here on a Wednesday at five o'clock. I, we, tried to call but we couldn't find a number."

"We have no telephone here," the old man said, smiling at Joe. "Why don't you put that chair down and join us," he said to Mr. Drew, and everyone was introduced to everyone else and everyone sat down and everyone, except Mildred, spoke, and the Drews listened carefully to everything that was said and they absorbed the sight of the beach and the sea, which was becoming more spectacular as the tide rose, and they looked very carefully at the old man and his friends and they looked at each other when Carl put his hand on the back of Lonny's chair, and they preserved it all for memory and analysis and retelling and amplification.

Gradually everyone's glass emptied, except Mildred's,

which had been drained almost as soon as she sat down, and this time instead of not offering any more the old man turned to Joe.

"I think we could use another bottle or two," he said, and Joe went into the house for more.

"Do you like it?" the old man asked the Drews.

"It's very good," Mrs. Drew said. "I always imagined that you'd drink champagne."

"I don't very often. Joe usually decides and he doesn't care for it much."

Mrs. Drew thought about that and her husband, who had been looking for the right opportunity, started the question he had come to ask.

"Your first book, *Magnificent Madness*, was beautifully written," he said, "but after that your books became more powerful, but darker and more pessimistic."

He waited for a word of agreement from the old man, but the old man did not like to talk about his writing and he said nothing. After a minute Mr. Drew went on.

"Then, nine or ten years ago, your work, even your stories in *The New Yorker,* became more cheerful and optimistic, and lighter. I've always wanted to know why."

Joe had returned with the champagne and had heard the end of the question, and he looked at the old man and the old man looked at him and they both smiled private smiles.

"More champagne, everyone?" Joe asked.

"Yes, please," the old man said. He stood up with his glass and then everyone stood up and held out theirs, except Mildred, who held out hers from her chair.

Mr. Drew had come a long way to ask his question and he was not willing to let the opportunity pass. He patted the hair over his bald spot nervously.

"Did something change in your life then?" he asked, "or did you just change your outlook?"

Elizabeth had been listening carefully. She knew that the

old man did not like to be questioned about his writing and she stepped forward and took his arm.

"He'd rather talk about reading than writing," she said to Mr. Drew. She patted the old man's hand.

"What have you been reading this summer?" she asked him before Mr. Drew could speak.

"Parts of the Old Testament, and some Gertrude Stein," the old man answered.

Mrs. Drew had been warned by her husband from the time they had first planned the trip that she must not mention one subject to the old man, and he had warned her again during the drive to Long Island, and again on the ferry over when she had stared at male passengers who were openly affectionate with each other, but the unnaturalness of sitting on the deck of Oswald Stevenson's beach house drinking champagne with him and the repetitiveness of her husband's warnings and the shock of the number of young men she had seen all combined to make her say the one thing she did not want to say, and before she knew it or could stop it she said vehemently:

"Gertrude Stein. That old dyke!"

Even the old man, who was usually unruffleable, was surprised and a little embarrassed, not at the word but because the comment had been unexpected and because he was concerned for the feelings of his friends, and for a brief time neither the old man nor anyone else knew what to say. Mr. Drew reddened and his wife looked as though she might cry. Then Lonny laughed, and Elizabeth laughed, and the bad moment started to pass and both Mr. Drew and his wife tried to apologize and they did not look directly at Elizabeth or Mildred.

"That's OK," Elizabeth said, "I guess she was an old dyke."

"You met her, didn't you?" she said to the old man.

The old man nodded but he did not yet smile, and then Mildred laughed, a little too loudly, and the old man did smile.

"Joe's easier to talk to about his work," Elizabeth said. "What are you working on?" she asked Joe as she sat down.

Everyone sat down and again Carl put his hand on the back of Lonny's chair. The old man was relieved that attention was on Joe, not himself.

"Just an article about Alexander the Great," Joe said.

"Now come on, it's more interesting than that," Carl said.

"Well, it's about his battle tactics—what was already known at his time and what he originated."

"They couldn't have been very complex, could they," Mr. Drew said. "He didn't have much to work with except large numbers, did he?"

"Actually he had quite a bit. Right now I'm writing about how he used the soldiers armed with sarissas. A sarissa was a kind of spear that wasn't thrown."

"Weren't they pretty long?" Carl asked.

"I'll say. Some of them were as long as eighteen feet, and the point was a foot-long blade."

"I'd hate to be shaved with that," Lonny said.

"I'll bet you would. When the sarissa carriers charged they held the sarissas down in front of themselves with two hands and swung them from side to side and roared out a war cry at the same time."

"Hell, I'd run," Carl said.

"Evidently a lot of people did."

Mildred held out her glass for more champagne and Joe emptied the bottle. He looked at the old man.

"I think a little more," the old man said, and Joe smiled and went for more. It was an unusual Afternoon.

When he returned the old man was talking to Mildred and Lonny was talking to the Drews, and Joe smiled fondly at the old man and put the bottle on the table. He sat across their semicircle from Carl and Elizabeth.

27

"Why did you pick Alexander?" Carl asked across the table.

"Because he was so young and he achieved military and political successes that people his age in our time couldn't imagine. He conquered all of the world he knew."

"If I remember correctly, he was pretty ruthless, wasn't he? Didn't he always kill his captives?"

"Sometimes," Joe said.

The old man looked up from his conversation with Mildred. "He says it doesn't matter."

"Now don't start that again," Joe said. He had drunk two or three glasses of champagne and he spoke more loudly than usual. He was not harsh, but he was not tender either.

"Did you know that even Freud wrote about Alexander?" Elizabeth said quickly.

Joe nodded. "He wrote about his dreams. Alexander once dreamed that there was a satyr dancing on his shield. He was besieging Tyre at the time." Joe looked over at the old man. "And Aristander interpreted his dream by rearranging the letters of the Greek word for satyr into the words 'Tyre is yours.' Aristander then predicted that Alexander would conquer Tyre, which he did. Freud's comments aren't very valuable."

Joe spoke to the old man, gently this time.

"You would like what Erasmus wrote. He wrote that Alexander was a miserable little man who disturbed and subjugated the world."

The old man did not answer, but he smiled.

"I wouldn't mind being Alexander," Lonny said.

"Me either," Joe said. "He was worshiped as a god, you know." He looked over at the old man again.

The Drews, chastened by their previous attempts at conversation, were clinging to their glasses and sitting quietly. Now Mr. Drew saw an opportunity.

"Saint Augustine wrote about Alexander too," he said.

"I know," Joe said. "In the *City of God*."

Mr. Drew looked disappointed.

"You'd like what he wrote too," Joe said to the old man.

"Not bad," the old man said. It was a compliment and Joe smiled because he knew that the old man was pleased and he liked to please the old man.

They finished the bottle of champagne and sat watching the waves that were growing ever higher and watching the people on the beach watching the waves, and they were quiet. They listened to the sound of the sea. The waves broke heavily in front of the house, and under the crash of the individual waves was an unending low roar. This time the old man did not suggest more champagne.

A policeman came riding up the beach on a dune bike with three large wheels for the sand. He came from the direction of the Pines, the next town to the east, and he skidded and turned into a stop facing them. The policeman was younger than Joe, and he enjoyed riding on the beach.

"Hello," he called.

Joe got up and went to the rail.

"Hi."

"Do you want that ride I promised you?" the policeman called up.

"Not now. How about tomorrow?" Joe said.

"Fine with me."

"No, wait. I can't then, I'll be in the city. How about Friday?"

"OK," the policeman called. He started his bike. "See you later," he called. "So long, Mr. Stevenson." He started off. "Have a nice trip," he called back.

They watched him disappear down the beach. "I bought him a couple of drinks the other night and he promised me a ride on his bike," Joe said. "He said I shouldn't call you Old Man," he said to the old man.

"How'd you get a name like Oswald anyway?" Mildred asked suddenly, turning toward the group.

The old man laughed. "My mother gave it to me."

"Sadistic woman," Mildred said.

"No, not really. It was my grandfather's name. My mother's father."

Joe had known the old man for ten years and although he had come to know him very well he still did not have a completely clear picture of the old man's past. It was not that the old man wanted to hide anything but that he did not like to talk about himself. Joe usually did not press the old man for details because he loved the old man and did not want to make him uncomfortable, but sometimes when the old man did seem willing to talk Joe asked a little.

"Did you know your grandfather?" he asked now.

"Yes," the old man said. "He came to live with us when I was around five and he lived with us until he died, when I was eight or nine. That was when we lived on the farm in Pennsylvania."

The old man looked up and far out to sea, and he looked beyond the sea and he remembered, with difficulty, a portly old man with white hair and a white beard and a large white mustache who spoke with a thick German accent.

"He was born in Germany," the old man said, "and he didn't come over here until my mother was thirteen or fourteen years old." The old man smiled at a memory. "When he lived with us he grew his own tobacco in a little garden out back. He hung the leaves from the rafters of an old shed to dry and I'd stand inside the shed and look at the sun coming in through the spaces between the boards on the sides and I'd smell the tobacco drying. It smelled sweet and brown."

The old man did not speak for a minute and no one else, not even Mildred, spoke either, and then he spoke again.

"Mother didn't want him to smoke in the house and she wouldn't let him smoke in the front where the neighbors could see him, so as long as the weather was good he sat in an old wooden kitchen chair on the ground by the back door and smoked his pipe. In the winter, or when it rained, he was allowed to smoke in the back of the kitchen by the stove. It was a wood-burning stove you know, and he'd bring in his old chair and sit by the stove smoking his pipe."

The old man stopped, and he watched the sea.

"Go on," Joe said.

The old man was quiet for a minute or two, and then continued. "He made his own beer. Mother always called it root beer, but it sure smelled strong and I was never allowed to taste it. He made it in the shed where he hung his tobacco, and I remember he used the same bottles over and over again. Sometimes they exploded and the brown beer would drip down the walls, and then he'd yell in German."

The old man chuckled a little.

"I remember when I had just found out about Darwin and I told everyone at home that our ancestors were apes. Grandfather got upset and said that maybe my relatives were monkeys but his weren't, and mother told me to go to my room.

"You know," the old man said, "even back then I was writing. I kept a notebook."

The old man seemed as if he might continue, but Mildred was not very good at sitting quietly listening to someone else talk unless she had a drink in her hand, and no one was going for more champagne.

"I'm hungry," she said. "Christ, it must be after six."

"I guess it is," the old man said, and he stood up and then everyone stood up.

"I'm going to the room," Mildred announced. "I know where it is." She went into the house and the old man and Elizabeth moved away from the others and talked quietly. Joe talked with the Drews for a few minutes while Lonny and Carl took the glasses to the kitchen and washed them and came back out and then the old man and Elizabeth came back to where Joe was standing and everyone said how nice it had been to see everyone else and the Drews apologized again and Elizabeth said "Don't worry," and they looked relieved and Joe said that they were welcome to come again and they smiled, and everyone moved around the house toward the gate except Elizabeth who went inside for Mildred.

The Drews said good-bye solemnly.

"Come again," the old man said. He had found them amusing and not too tiring and he thought that they probably had more to offer than they had showed.

"We will," they said, and then Lonny gave the old man and Joe each a hug and Carl said "See ya" to Joe and "Good-bye" to the old man, and the four left together.

Mildred and Elizabeth came around the house.

"Why don't you come back Saturday," the old man told them. He put his arm around Mildred's shoulders.

"Maybe we will," Elizabeth said.

Joe did not mind Elizabeth, although he did not know her very well, but he was not looking forward to the return of Mildred. Since Joe had known the old man, Joe and Mildred had always treated each other warily, and Mildred always called him "kid," which angered him.

"Bye kid," Mildred said to Joe, and then everyone said good-bye. Joe closed the gate, and Joe and the old man were alone again.

"Well?" Joe said. He meant should they leave then for an early dinner or should they rest for a while, and the old man knew it.

"I don't think a little more champagne would hurt," the old man said. "It'll be high tide shortly. We could sit out and watch it."

"We've both had quite a bit, you know. What about work tomorrow?"

"Ah, tomorrow. I never get a lot done when you're not around anyway. I'll start a little later in the morning and work through part of the afternoon."

"OK," Joe said, and they went into the kitchen for glasses and champagne and walked through the front room and out onto the deck facing the sea. The waves were tremendous and when they broke the water came more than halfway across the upper beach to the dunes.

"They'll wash up to the dunes in a few minutes. Should be quite a show," the old man said. They drew two of the canvas chairs up to the rail and sat and watched the sea and drank champagne.

"You know, I've had about enough of Mildred," Joe said. "I never did like women who were drunks, and on top of that she's loud and rude. And she's mean."

"How about men who are drunks?"

"Come on. I'm talking about Mildred."

"She's old," the old man said.

"Yes, and so are you, but you aren't mean."

They did not look at each other as they spoke, but they looked at the sea.

"I've had my days," the old man said. "I used to make people in my classes cry."

"I know. That's one of the reasons I signed up; I wanted to see what the great S.O.B. was like. You didn't make me cry."

"Most people aren't as manipulative as you are."

The old man turned to Joe and smiled. He was not trying to be mean, but both of them knew that Joe had an inexplicable, sometimes unconscious ability to make people do what he wanted them to do. They had talked about it often when Joe had been younger, and the old man had called it a gift and had said that Joe should try to find some way of using it constructively. Joe had; he was an excellent professor and managed to motivate his students to do unusual amounts of work.

"Anyway," the old man said, "you should be more kind to Mildred. Elizabeth told me she has cancer, and she only has a year or two."

33

"God, that's too bad. They're almost always together, what will Elizabeth do?"

"I don't know," said the old man. "I've known her for almost thirty years and she's been with Mildred since I've known her."

"Thirty years? How did you meet her, anyway?"

"She was my psychiatrist."

"Psychiatrist! I've known you for ten years and I never knew you had seen a shrink."

"There's a lot you don't know," the old man said, and he stood up. "Look. I was right." He pointed to a wet line on the sand where seconds before a wave had washed up to the snow fence on the dunes. "Isn't that some sea? It's a good thing there's not a full moon tonight or the tide might come up to the house."

"I wish you'd spend some time recording your memories," Joe said to the old man. "I really do want to write your biography some day."

"There'll be time for that when I'm old," the old man said. "Come on, let's go over and watch the sunset before dinner. We can just leave this stuff here."

And the old man and the young man left the barely touched champagne and walked around the house and did not think about locking the door and they walked out the gate and toward the bay, where there was an upstairs bar with a view of the sunset. When they reached the bar they sat outside on the balcony and watched the sun as it sank toward the horizon. A little above the horizon was a thin line of purple clouds and when the sun went below the clouds the air was cooler and the sky was darker, but then they saw a little gleam of orange and slowly the sun came out, and then it colored the clouds and the surrounding sky so brightly orange that looking at it was like looking into the interior of a fiery blast furnace.

They left when the sun touched the horizon. A breeze came up, and as the two of them, the old man and the young man, walked to the restaurant the breeze blew their long hair, white and red-brown, about their faces.

The same maître d' had been at the restaurant for many years. He had been there the summer that Joe had first come to the island. The old man, who had come to the island before Joe, could remember a time when the maître d' had not been there, but the restaurant had not been there either. The maître d', whose name was Robert—no one called him Bob but some people called him the Duchess—always wore a floor-length caftan and often wore a long string of gaudy beads. He knew everyone who lived in the Grove and all of the residents knew him, and he always had a friendly greeting for everyone he saw, except Mildred, who had once grabbed his beads and slapped his face. Joe and the old man always came to say hello to him when they arrived on the island for the summer and always they said good-bye before they left.

"Hello there," Robert said. "How was your Afternoon? Carl said he stopped over."

Carl tended bar in the restaurant and they could see him working.

"We had fun," the old man replied.

"What'd you think of Carl's new friend?" Robert asked.

Joe and the old man both smiled. "He's sweet," Joe said.

"I give it two weeks," Robert said, "but that's life. Carl said Mildred was her usual sweet self."

"Isn't she always?" Joe asked.

"Someone ought to put that woman out of her misery."

"She's old," Joe said. "But the hell with Mildred. How about some dinner? Will you take a couple of hungry walk-ins?"

"We'll always have room for you," Robert told him. "Table for two for Walter Irving," he said to a younger man who was seating people. The initials W. I. stood for walk-in.

"Go ahead," Joe said to the old man. "I want to talk to

35

Carl for a minute," and the old man followed the young man with the menus and Joe went to the bar. Carl rang up a sale and put some money in the register and some in a glass at the side, and then he came over to where Joe was standing.

"What'd you think of Lonny?" Carl asked.

"He's sweet," Joe said. "Listen. Could you do a favor for me?"

"Sure. What?"

"You know I'm going to the city tomorrow?"

"Yeah."

"Well, could you stop in tomorrow afternoon for a while to keep the old man company? I know I'm just going to be gone for the day, but I think he gets lonesome. And then, even though he knows I won't be back until evening, he'll start watching for me around two or three and he'll just sit out on the deck and wait."

"Sure, I'll go over. We'll go swimming or something."

"Thanks. Want anything from the city?"

"I'll take Cartier's if you're offering."

"No, seriously, can I bring anything back for you?"

"No, I guess not. Thanks anyway."

"OK," Joe said. "We'll say good-bye before we leave."

He went back to where Robert was standing. "Where'd you put us?" he asked, and Robert told him, and he joined the old man. There was a bottle of champagne in an ice bucket beside the table.

"I've ordered for us," the old man said as Joe sat down.

"You know," Joe told him, "neither of us is going to walk very well tonight, and you're not going to work well tomorrow."

"We haven't had that much," the old man said. "Besides, we've both been working hard and we need a little relaxation."

Joe pulled the bottle out of the ice and looked at the label. "Dom Perignon! This book you're writing better sell."

Joe put the bottle back into the ice and took a sip from his glass, which the old man had already filled.

"I'll bet I live better than Alexander did," Joe said.

"Probably. But I'm not sure Alexander was interested in good living; he was more comfortable on the battlefield."

The old man drank some champagne. "What was that dream you were talking to Elizabeth about again?"

"You know, during the siege of Tyre Alexander dreamed of a satyr dancing on his shield."

"Considering the fate of some of the citizens of Tyre, a cross would have been more appropriate than a shield. What did a shield have to do with it, anyway?"

"I don't know. Ask Elizabeth," Joe said.

Their soup came—a creamy chowder thick with clams, and they ate it while they talked.

"Do you remember this afternoon I told you that you would like what Saint Augustine wrote about Alexander?" Joe asked.

"I may be old, but I'm not senile. What did he write?"

"He retold the story of Alexander and the pirate. A pirate was brought to Alexander, and Alexander asked him why he infested the sea. The pirate told Alexander that he infested the sea for the same reason Alexander infested the earth but because he used a little ship he was called a pirate and because Alexander used a large army and navy he was called an emperor."

"Three cheers for the pirate. I'll bet he regretted that remark."

"I don't know. Alexander probably let him go."

Their conversation turned from Alexander to Tamerlane, who had followed part of Alexander's route across the Hindu Kush, and then they talked about Pentheus in *The Bacchae,* whose mother tore him apart while she was in a bacchanalian frenzy, and then the waiter came to take away their soup bowls.

"How was it, boys?" he asked.

"Fine," they both answered, and they resumed their conversation before the waiter moved away.

Joe poured more champagne.

"I've been thinking about Alexander for a couple of years now, and I still can't answer one question," he said. "Why? What made a twenty-year-old leave his home and set out to conquer the world? You know, he campaigned for ten years and he never made it back to Macedonia. And he never saw his mother again either."

"Youth, as we both know, is impetuous," the old man said. He was remembering a time when Joe had been twenty. "He probably wouldn't have done it if he'd been older. Of course, it's possible that he just didn't like Macedonia."

Joe laughed. "It's possible. A hundred years earlier Socrates was given the opportunity to flee to Macedonia and he said it was better to die in Athens than to live in Macedonia."

They both laughed, and their meal arrived and they talked on. The restaurant was crowded. During dinner the sounds around them rose and fell like waves, an occasional voice piercing the wash of sound and becoming momentarily intelligible and then fading away; waiters obtruded then withdrew; tanned, well-cared-for bodies approached and passed and faded into the background, glanced at then forgotten; the disco in the front room laid a throbbing foundation to the waves of sound; someone at a nearby table pleaded against an already consummated rejection; and Joe and the old man talked about Alexander and about writing and about Mildred and about Lonny, and then they were through and the old man signed the check and for them it was late.

On the way out they spoke to Carl and Robert, and they stood a minute in the disco and watched the moving bodies and then they walked through and out into the night. They walked up the boardwalk toward the sea, but instead of turning on the walk that led to their house they continued toward the sea until they were at the top of a flight of steps that led down to the beach from the top of the dunes.

"Let's sit for a few minutes," the old man said, and they sat on the steps and watched the sea. The night was dark and there was no moon. The sky was cloudless and the stars were brilliant. They picked out the jagged line of bright stars of Cassiopeia. They would not see the waves as they swelled, but when the waves started to crest they could see a line of white start and extend quickly, parallel to the beach, and then fall into white foam. Sometimes two white lines started and raced toward each other and then joined as the wave broke.

"You know," Joe said, "my brother's got to see this. This makes Lake Michigan look like a bathtub."

"I don't think your parents would let him come here."

"He's twenty," Joe said. "He doesn't need their permission."

"That's true," the old man answered. He did not turn away from the sea. "But they could make it very unpleasant for him."

"I know. I don't understand why he's living at home. He could have gone to college wherever he wanted to, and he picked Evanston."

"Maybe he didn't want to leave," the old man said.

"I think that after me my father is afraid to let him out of his sight."

They watched the sea silently. Joe was remembering a time, ten years ago, when he and the old man had gone to Evanston. His parents had been happy that their son was renting a room in Oswald Stevenson's house, and they were proud when Joe asked if he could bring the man home with him for Thanksgiving, and if they thought anything about it being strange they told themselves that the man did not have a family of his own and everyone knows families are nice on holidays.

Joe remembered making the old man come, and that

made him a little sad now, and he remembered telling his family how things were with him and the old man, and he remembered that his father and the old man had shut themselves in a room and shouted, and then he and the old man had left and then, as now, Joe was proud of the old man and although then he had not been proud of himself, now he was proud of himself too.

The old man was thinking about satyrs.

"Sometimes you're like a satyr," he said after they had been quiet for a while.

"Me?" Joe laughed. "How about you? You write books and live the life of leisure. I have to work. Besides," he added jokingly, "you look a little like a goat."

The old man laughed. "Maybe. But it's easier to imagine you dancing naked in a woodland meadow than me."

"Do you know what Alexander did when he visited Troy?" Joe asked.

"No."

"He stripped, rubbed himself with oil, and ran naked through the streets carrying a wreath to leave at Achilles's tombstone. His lover Hephaestion did the same for another of the heroes of the *Iliad*."

"I can certainly imagine you doing that."

"Me too. Come on, let's go home. We can walk down the beach." Joe got up and held out his hand to the old man.

They walked down the steps to the sand and walked on the sand toward their house. They carried their shoes and walked in the hard wet sand below the high tide line. The sound made by the pieces of shell and tiny stones tumbling in the waves seemed louder in the darkness than it had during the day; it was no longer the quiet clicking of tiny bamboo wind chimes being stirred by a gentle breeze but was a steady hiss.

The evening had grown cool, as August evenings sometimes do, and the old man shivered.

"I hate fall," he said suddenly. "It's nature's dirty little trick. Everything looks so colorful and so splendid, and everything is dying."

"You've always loved the fall," Joe said.

"I was younger then." The old man shivered again.

"It's Mildred, isn't it?"

"Partly," said the old man.

The coolness of the evening made the old man aware of the passing of the seasons, and he knew that he was old and wished that he were young, and he felt helpless and sad.

"Have you ever thought of writing poetry?" Joe asked.

"No. What does that have to do with fall?"

"You could write a long, obscure poem about fall and begin it with 'Autumn is the cruellest time.'"

"That's not funny. And I don't think Eliot would appreciate it," the old man said, but as he spoke the sudden sadness dissipated.

They walked down the beach without speaking. The old man was thinking about time and Joe was thinking about poetry.

"You know," the old man said suddenly, "time is funny. We experience it like a long string being pulled slowly through our fingers, but we remember it bunched together like beads." He stopped and looked up. "Or like the stars. Some things we remember brightly and other things not at all, and then we rearrange everything. Those stars in Cassiopeia could represent events that happened years apart but are remembered together in one bright line."

Joe thought about that. "What are your most vivid memories? Happy ones?" he asked.

"Well, that weekend you came to New York I guess, and publishing my first book. And I guess I'd have to say—no, never mind."

"You guess you'd have to say what?"

"Some other time," the old man said.

They were almost home. They could see their house ahead of them and the dark shape of the steps over the dunes.

"You could use a day away from work," Joe said. "Why don't you come with me tomorrow?"

"No, I'd rather stay out here and watch the sea."

"You might change your mind in the morning," Joe said as they climbed the steps, but the old man knew he would not, and the old man and the young man walked around the house and went through the door to the kitchen.

"I'm tired," the old man said when they got in.

"Go on to bed," Joe told him. "I'm going to sit up for a while, and I've got to clean up."

And Joe sat at his desk and wrote down his poem about the fall, and then he wrote a little about Alexander until the old man was ready for bed and had climbed the winding steps to the loft.

"Good night," the old man called down.

"I'll be up soon," Joe said, and he turned out the light on his desk so the old man could sleep and he went out on the deck to listen to the waves and watch the lines of foam and look at the stars, and he thought about the old man, and fall, and the passing of time, and Mildred, and Alexander, and he understood things that many other young men do not. After he sat for a while he picked up the bottle and glasses that they had left on the table earlier and went inside and, after he cleaned the kitchen and measured the coffee and water for the morning, he got ready for bed and climbed the steps and lay down beside the old man, and he turned and put his arm around the old man and brought himself up against the old man's back. Above him, through the skylight, he could see the stars, and in the dim light the old man looked old and a little frail, and the lines on his face were filled with shadows, and as Joe faded into sleep he thought about making love with the old man, and he thought about all of the young men he had made love with in the past ten years and he thought that, after all those years, he still loved the old man more.

Joe and the old man slept, and while they slept the old man dreamed of satyrs dancing in the distance on the beach. In his dream he walked to watch the satyrs dance and as he came closer the satyrs gradually metamorphosed into sleek, darkly tanned young men with red-brown hair and, as the old man watched, their hair started to glow and soon the old man had to look away because the young men's hair became as bright as the interior of a fiery blast furnace, or the setting sun. He smiled in his sleep and Joe slept quietly beside him.

The old man awoke early, as he always did. Above him, over the skylight, the sky was dark purple, almost black, but through the side windows he could see the sky turning pink in the east. He lay in the bed and watched while the eastern sky turned peach-colored and then orange, and the sky above him grew lighter and the stars faded and then went out, and when the pink blush reached the sky overhead he got up. He got up quietly because Joe was still sleeping and as he got up he felt the beginning throb of a headache and his throat felt dry and his mouth tasted bad. He put on his robe and went down into the kitchen and turned on the coffee maker and, as he did every morning, while the coffee maker was making coffee and while Joe was still sleeping, he showered. His voice was rough and he hardly sang at all.

When he got out of the shower and was dry he put his robe back on and went into the kitchen and poured two cups of coffee and carried them up to the loft. He held one of the cups near Joe's face and fanned the steam toward him with his hand.

"Good morning!"

Joe was already awake, but he wished that he was not.

43

"Good morning, hell." He sat up and took the coffee. "Now I remember why I don't like champagne."

"You can't feel that bad," the old man said. "You didn't have that much."

"Christ," Joe said. "Of all the people to live with, I had to choose Bacchus reincarnated."

Joe put the coffee on a table by the bed, stood up, and put on a robe that the old man threw to him.

"I am not making breakfast," he said. "Either you're cooking or we're going out." He started down the steps with his coffee. "And now I'm going to be late getting into the city, too."

"Let's go out," the old man said.

"Fine. You're paying," Joe called up.

The pot of coffee was gone and it was almost seven-thirty before they left. They walked down the boardwalk toward the center of the Grove and enjoyed the morning. Joe wore long pants, a polo shirt, and shoes, and the old man wore white shorts and a T-shirt saying "Cherry Grove" and sandals. Because their hair was still a little damp it did not blow about their faces in the breeze.

They ate breakfast at a restaurant that overlooked the sea. That season it was known for its layer cakes coated thickly with frosting and decorated with candies, and it had a large fireplace that was never used. The only other customers were two policemen, and they waved.

"Good morning," the younger one called. He was the one who had offered Joe the ride on the dune bike. His name was Bob, and he was never called Robert.

"Good morning," Joe and the old man each said, and they sat at a table from which they could see the sea and that was across the end of the room from the policemen.

"I saw Carl last night," Bob called across to them. "He said you two were still drinking champagne at the restaurant at nine o'clock. How do you feel?"

44

"Four out of ten," Joe said. "It's his fault." He pointed at the old man.

"The devil made me do it," the old man said.

Everyone laughed and the policemen resumed their conversation. Joe and the old man watched the sea. It was calm, and brilliant with the morning sun.

A waitress came over with two cups of coffee. "Morning guys," she said as the put down the cups. "Would you like breakfast?"

Joe and the old man ordered a substantial breakfast because they had formed the habit of not eating lunch in the summer, and they watched the sea and drank the coffee while they waited for the food to arrive.

"Did you dream about the beach last night?" Joe asked the old man.

As sometimes when you have driven a long distance and that night dream about driving, or when you have traveled for hours in a train and then dream about trains so, after he had spent part of the day on the beach in the sun, the old man often dreamed about beaches. The dreams did not start in May, when he first came to the island for the summer, but as June passed and the days became hotter and brighter and the water became warmer the old man began to dream of endless beaches and perfect skies and translucent seas, and for the rest of the summer most of his dreams included a beach. The dreams continued for a while in the fall when they returned to the city and only came to the island on weekends, but as the fall went on and the air grew cooler and the days shortened the dreams became more and more infrequent and then ceased. Occasionally, though, deep in January or February he would again dream of a beach, and then it was usually not a northern beach but a tropical beach where white sand sparkled around a horseshoe-shaped lagoon of blue-green water in which fish passed lazily through forests of seaweed and extravagant gardens of coral. The beach would be lined with kumquat trees and palms and the old man would hear the callings of tropical birds, and he would long for the sea. Then, sometimes, the old man and the young man would pack and go south for a long weekend, or longer if Joe could get away from teaching. They would not go to Key West, where they usually went for winter vacations, but far beyond to the shores of Barbados or Tobago or South America or, twice, to the South Pacific.

But now they were on Fire Island, and as they sat watching the Atlantic the old man told Joe about his dream. Joe had always found the old man's dreams fascinating and he speculated about their meanings. He had once told the old man that he should write accounts of his dreams and publish them, but the old man had said no he wrote fiction not psychology and besides, he had said, our dreams are our most private possessions. But the old man also agreed with Joe that perhaps his ability to write had something to do with his ability to dream.

The waitress brought their breakfast and set it down not too gently in front of them. "How's writing going?" she asked the old man, and the old man said that it was going fine just fine.

"You're going to have to go to work again pretty soon," she said to Joe, and he said yes, and that it was too bad the summer was ending and that in fact he was going to his office that day. And then the waitress went away and the policemen said good-bye and left and the two of them were alone in the room. They talked about the old man's dream and about satyrs and then Joe asked the old man about his work.

"Are you going to work today?" he asked.

"I've been thinking about just relaxing for the day," the old man said. He paused and looked at the sea. "I've been trying to read the Old Testament. This might be a good day to work at it."

"Then if you're not going to work, why don't you come with me?" Joe asked. He leaned over the table toward the old man as he spoke.

"I hate to leave here if I don't have to. September's coming soon enough and then there'll be only weekends, and then pretty soon we'll have to close up."

The waitress came with more coffee and then left.

"Besides, you know I don't like traffic," the old man said.

"I don't know why that bothers you. You just follow the road and you get there."

"I know," said the old man, but he was not going.

Joe wanted the old man to come with him but he knew that the old man would not, and he played with his spoon.

"You know, Alexander probably never would have found Persepolis, much less conquered it, if it hadn't been for the Persian royal highway."

"What?" The old man looked away from the sea.

"Alexander didn't have a map and the only descriptions he had were old and inaccurate. He didn't really know where he was going, but when he found the royal highway he followed it all the way to Persepolis and conquered everything along the way." Joe finished the rest of his coffee in one swallow and pushed the cup and saucer away. "And speaking of highways, I'd better catch the ferry so I can get on one."

The old man agreed, and they stood up and the waitress brought the check and the old man paid it.

"I'll walk you to the ferry," he said.

"You don't have to. I'll probably have to wait and then you might have to deal with the tourists."

The old man was often recognized from his photographs and was known by many to live on the island in the summer, and when he went to the dock, which was by the big hotel, he was sometimes stopped by strangers who wanted to talk about his books or about their books or sometimes about Joe or who sometimes just wanted to be able to say that they had met him. The old man wanted to wait with Joe, but the effects of the champagne did not make him eager to meet strangers and he agreed that he would not go to the ferry. He said he was going to take a walk.

They parted on the boardwalk by the restaurant.

"See you tonight," Joe said.

"You too," the old man replied.

The old man started up the steps that led down over the dunes and Joe walked in the opposite direction toward the ferry.

"Hey!" Joe called back to the old man. The old man stopped and turned around.

"Carl might stop by this afternoon. Give him a drink or something," Joe called.

"I will," the old man called back, and with a wave he disappeared down the steps to the beach.

Joe followed the boardwalk to the dock. The ferry was not there yet, but he could see it coming across Great South Bay. He had a few minutes so he walked and looked in the windows of the shops, and when he came to the flower shop, Bloominpails, he went inside.

"Hi there," he said to the young man in the shop.

"Hi Joe," the young man said. "Going to the city?" he asked, noting Joe's clothes.

"Unfortunately. But I'm coming back tonight."

The young man was unpacking bird of paradise flowers that had come in on an earlier freight boat.

"Did you see the waves last night?" he asked.

"I sure did. They were the best of the season." Joe picked up one of the flowers. "How much are the birds?"

The young man told him and Joe asked for a dozen.

"Can you take them to the house?" he asked.

"Sure. I'll do it now. How's the old man?"

"He's not getting any younger," Joe said, "but he's fine, just fine." As Joe spoke he realized that he spoke a little like the old man did and he smiled.

The young man nodded while he fixed the flowers.

48

"Do you want a card or anything with them?" he asked.

"No thanks. He'll know who sent them," Joe said. "But if you go over there now he might not be there, so just leave them on the bench by the kitchen door."

"Sure will," the young man said, and Joe paid him and they both said thank you and good-bye and Joe returned to the dock where the ferry was tying up. As he waited to board he saw the young man from Bloominpails lock the shop and head up the walk with a large bunch of flowers wrapped in paper.

Meanwhile, the old man had been walking. He walked down the beach in the direction he had swum the day before with Joe, and as he walked he looked at the water marks on the dunes and he thought about the sea. The sea was calm; the water came in slow, undulating swells that gathered themselves up in the last instant before they reached the beach and then fell onto the sand with a soft slap.

He walked to the forest where he had walked with Joe, and as he climbed the steps over the dunes he noticed that the waves had washed over the patch of sea rocket and that bits of debris had been left clinging to the plant. Although the delicate blossoms had survived, the old man thought that the plant would soon die from the salt. The old man followed the boardwalk through the woods, enjoying the saltsmell combined with the smell of the woods and enjoying the feel of the boardwalk under his feet, and he came to the place where they had seen the dead gull. Feathers were still scattered on the deck but now the gull was out under the trees.

Again the old man thought of the gull's dying moments and in the quiet woods he could hear the screaming of the bird and the snarling of the animal killing it, and then he heard the moist sounds of the animal eating its kill and the crunch of teeth on bone and the snap of teeth on teeth, and he imagined the animal finishing its meal, giving the carcass a sniff, and running off happily through the trees. It reminded him of Alexander. He shuddered and left the place quickly.

He took a path back through the woods that led to a high point from which he could see the dunes and the ocean beyond them on one side and across the island to the bay on the other side. Both the ocean and the bay were brilliantly blue, and the blue of the bay was spotted with white sails. The old man sat on a bench in the warm sun and thought about the previous day. When he remembered the Drews he laughed.

"Well, she was an old dyke," he said aloud, and he remembered the two times he had met her. The first time had been at the Algonquin in New York when she was lecturing in America after the success of her *Autobiography of Alice B. Toklas*. Miss Stein was discovering herself as a real celebrity and she acted regally toward the young Oswald, who at the time was an almost unknown writer, but she invited him to visit her in Paris as she invited everybody in America. Perhaps she felt safe inviting so many people to see her in Paris because an ocean separated America from Europe, but many people did visit her, including the old man. The old man imagined Mrs. Drew meeting Miss Toklas and he laughed. Miss Toklas had not always been very pleasant and had sometimes been fierce.

At the same time he was remembering the Misses Stein and Toklas the old man noted that he was remembering the past and he thought that spending more time remembering the past must be a part of growing old. When he was with Joe he thought mostly about the present and the future, but when he was alone he increasingly thought about the past. And so he sat in the sun and thought about Gertrude Stein and Alice Toklas and Mrs. Drew, and he thought about Joe, and more than an hour passed.

He might have stayed longer but a young man and a young woman who were holding hands appeared on the walk. They stopped and looked at the old man sitting on the bench

50

and then they stood a little way up the walk and the young man leaned back against the rail and the young woman leaned into him and they embraced tightly. The old man stood up and followed the boardwalk down the hill. When he reached the bottom he was in a depression between the high place where he had just been and the high dunes toward the sea. He looked back and saw the young man and young woman huddled together on the bench where he had been sitting, and he climbed the steps over the dunes and descended to the sea.

He took off his sandals and walked in the water back in the direction from which he had come. While he walked he listened for the sound made by the pebbles and fragments of shell, but because there were almost no waves if there was any sound he could not hear it. He decided that he would write that day, and while he walked he tried to plan what he would write. Again and again his thoughts wandered away from his work and again and again he brought them back, and sometimes he mumbled to himself. And then he was near to their house and he stopped thinking about what he was going to write and thought about the things he would do before he wrote. As he walked toward the house he thought of a long list of things that needed to be done, and he knew that if Joe were working at his desk then he too would be working and not sweeping sand or moving books or changing sheets.

The old man climbed the steps by the house slowly and went through the gate. On the bench by the kitchen door was a large package, obviously flowers, and he picked it up and opened the top a little to see what they were. He smiled and went into the house. The house still smelled damp from the night before, and he left the flowers on the table in the kitchen and opened the windows in the kitchen and climbed to the loft and opened the windows there, and he opened the glass doors facing the sea.

He went back into the kitchen and put the flowers one by one into a vase. "Pretty birds," he said, and he remembered a place where bird of paradise flowers grew wild and where hibiscus of every color were everywhere, and he knew that Joe had sent the flowers and had remembered the same place when he had bought them. The old man put the vase of flowers on a low glass table along the wall opposite the loft in the front room.

The old man then sorted books and cleaned and made coffee and drank coffee, and almost an hour passed before he was ready to work. When he was ready he sat at his desk, took out his pen, his glasses, and a file folder filled with long yellow paper, and read what he had written the day before. Then he began to write quickly, but he did not write for long before he held his glasses in his hand and looked out to sea and let his eyes drift out of focus until he saw only a blur, and he thought about Joe. The old man thought about Joe as he had been the day before while he swam, and he thought about him when he had been a brash, mildly arrogant young man of twenty, and he thought about him now and about his teaching and his writing, and he was proud. Then he thought about otters again, as he had the day before, and he thought about how otters swim and dive and play in the water and about how sea otters float on their backs with their feet sticking up from the water and crack mollusks against a stone held on their chest, and he laughed. "You old goat," he said to himself, and he put on his glasses and started to work again.

And so the morning passed, and the old man alternately worked and daydreamed and remembered, and he missed the sound of the typewriter. He stopped early, not only because Joe was not there but also because he wanted to send something in the day's mail. When he stopped he read what he had written and he was not satisfied, but he knew that once it was on paper it could be worked with, and he knew that seldom was his writing bad enough to have to be discarded, and then he thought about Virginia Woolf, who had destroyed so much that she had written—even whole novels—and he wondered how she had done it. He thought that destroying a book after spending many months living with its characters would be like killing part of the family.

He finished re-reading his work and he put his papers in a folder and put the folder, his glasses, and his pen inside the top drawer of his desk and stood up. He stretched widely, facing the sea, and he picked up the envelope he wanted to mail. He looked on Joe's desk to see if he had anything to mail and he noticed that Joe had not opened the letter he had received the day before. In the middle of the desk was a paper with a poem on it and when the old man saw the title he picked it up and read it.

With Apologies To T. S. Eliot

Autumn is the cruellest time, dying
Leaves disguised with bright colors, rotting
Vegetation below, warning
The coming of winter.

The old man laughed and thought that it was a fair imitation, and he remembered meeting Eliot in London once. The old man had been surprised that Eliot was the person who had written the poetry he certainly had written. He caught himself remembering again and he shook his head and started out to mail his letter.

Fire Island is a long, narrow strip of sand with the open Atlantic on one side and Great South Bay on the other. In Cherry Grove there are only two boardwalks that extend the length of the town and run parallel to the sea and the bay, and they are joined by several short walks with names like Summer Walk and Holly Walk and Doctor's Walk. Usually the old man followed the walk that ran on the ocean side of the island into the center of the Grove, but this time he took one of the shorter walks across to the walk that ran along the bay because the walk that ran along the bay led directly to the post office. He posted his letter and he checked their box for mail, but there was none, and he continued on toward the stores. Joe usually did the shopping so the old man did not have to brave the tourists and daytrippers, but now the old man decided to buy some things himself.

He passed Bloominpails and the young man who had delivered the flowers came out.

"Hi there. Did you get the flowers?"

"I sure did," the old man said. "Did Joe send them?"

"Yeah. He said you'd know."

"I did, thanks. They're beautiful."

The young man said thank you and the old man started to continue on, but then he stopped and turned back.

"Why don't you come over sometime when you're not working?" he said to the young man, who was still standing in the door of the shop. "We usually have some wine around five on Wednesdays and Saturdays. Stop in."

"Thanks, I'd like that. Joe's asked me too, but I've never made it."

"Well, we'll look for you then," the old man said, and he went on to a store by the dock.

The clerk in the store knew him and he asked about Joe and the old man told him about Joe and he paid for his purchases and prepared to leave. While he had been talking to the clerk two young men dressed only in swimming trunks had been listening, and when he picked up his bag one of the young men spoke to him.

"Aren't you Oswald Stevenson?"

"Yes."

The old man was curt. He did not feel like talking to strangers and he wished that Joe were here to talk to them so he could stand and listen and not talk.

"See," the young man said to his companion. "I told you it was Oswald Stevenson."

54

"We saw your picture in *The New York Times Book Review* in March," he said to the old man.

The young man stopped and waited for the old man to say something. The old man was not sure what to say so he said thank you and started to leave.

"Wait," the young man said. "What did you think about what they wrote about your book, that one that takes place in Canada someplace?"

"Montreal."

"Yeah. That's the one."

"I don't read reviews of my books."

The old man did not think it was necessary to add that although he did not usually read reviews of his books Joe had read that review and they had discussed parts of it carefully. The review had said that as the old man grew older his books grew calmer and more gentle and, if the trend continued, sometime, if he lived long enough, he would write a book with no action at all but just a "gently undulating mental landscape."

The old man made a serious effort to leave the store, but the young man was persistent. He stood between the old man and the door.

"Can I buy you a drink?" he asked.

The old man was annoyed now.

"I suppose you can as long as you've got the money, but I won't be there to drink it. Now if you'd allow me to, I'd like to leave."

The young man, embarrassed, stood away from the door.

"I was just trying to be nice. You could at least be polite." He pouted a little and his friend looked at him comfortingly.

The old man left the shop without answering and without saying good-bye to the clerk and he walked down the boardwalk toward the center of the Grove thinking dark thoughts, and for the first time he wished he had gone to New York with Joe.

"Hey, smile!" one of Joe's friends said as he passed the old man, and the old man smiled although he did not mean it. However, as he walked through the town toward the sea he saw several people he knew and everyone had a friendly greeting and some asked about Joe, and the old man began to regret his impatience in the store. "Silly old fool," he said to himself, and he began to smile.

He met Carl at the intersection of two boardwalks near the restaurant where he and Joe had eaten breakfast that morning.

"How about some breakfast?" Carl asked.

"Breakfast. It's after one."

"It's breakfast for me. I worked late last night and was up even later."

The old man smiled. "Where's Lonny?"

"Sleeping, of course. Anyway, if you've had breakfast you can have lunch."

"Never touch it. Besides, I had too much champagne last night. I think I'm going to take a nap."

"Have fun—" Carl turned away from the old man to say hello to a young man passing by who looked curiously at the old man and Carl.

"That guy was in the restaurant last night. He came out here alone," Carl told the old man when he turned back.

"Another one searching for love?" the old man asked.

"Either that or trying to forget it."

The old man nodded. "Go on," he said. "Have your breakfast. You need it to keep up with Lonny."

"That I do," Carl answered. "I thought I might stop in later if that's all right," he added.

"It sure is. Joe said I might see you this afternoon."

"OK. I'll see you later then." Carl gave the old man's shoulder a pat.

The old man said good-bye and started down the walk that led to his house and ran parallel to the ocean.

"Bring Lonny," he called back.

"I will," Carl answered.

Carl went up to the restaurant and the old man continued home. The wind ruffled his hair and it was white in the sun. When he arrived home he went into the kitchen, put his bag on the table, poured himself a large glass of mineral water from a bottle in the refrigerator, and took two aspirin. He decided to nap on the deck and he took off his shirt and went outside. There were two folded lounge chairs leaning against the side of the house and he carried one around and opened it where he could see the sea. He could hear the soft slap of the waves and the sounds of the people on the beach and occasionally the calling and squabbling of gulls, and then he slept.

He slept for more than two hours and if he dreamed he did not remember it. He would have slept longer if he had not heard Carl's voice. Carl was at the kitchen door and the old man heard him through the house and around the house.

"Hello! Anybody home!" Carl called through the door.

"I'm out here. Come on through."

The old man sat up. He was stiff from the lounge chair. Carl came out as the old man was stretching.

"I guess I woke you. I'm sorry."

"Don't be, I'm not. What time is it anyway?" The old man stretched again and looked out at the sea.

"A little after three-thirty, I think." Carl did not wear a watch in the summer because he did not want a band on his wrist that was not tanned.

"Either I'm getting old, or I had too much champagne last night. Or both." The old man laughed. "Come in and make yourself a drink if you want one," he said. "I'm going to take a shower to wake up."

The old man motioned to Carl to precede him and the two of them went through the front room and into the kitchen.

57

"Help yourself. You know where everything is," the old man said, and he went into the bathroom.

Carl made himself a gin and tonic and sat at the kitchen table drinking it. He heard the shower start, and then he heard the old man begin to sing. He sang an aimless song that drifted off into nothing, but then after a brief silence he started into something from *Carmen* with his full voice. Carl laughed, and he drank his gin and tonic.

The old man came out with a towel around his waist. "I'm going to put on some fresh things," he said. "Why don't you go out on the deck where it's pleasant? I'll be down in a minute."

"May I make you a drink?"

"No thanks. I'm sticking to Perrier." The old man went into the front room and up to the loft.

"Where's Lonny?" he called down as Carl passed through the front room on his way to the deck.

"Out somewhere working on his tan. He said he'd stop by later."

"That'll be nice," the old man said.

Carl went out onto the deck and sat in one of the canvas chairs and watched the sea. In front of the house two men and two children, a boy and a girl, were sunbathing naked on the beach. They were all very tanned, and the children and one of the men had light blond hair. The blond man lay with his arm across the back of his dark-haired friend. Far beyond them, near the horizon, Carl could see a ship faintly shimmering in the sun.

The old man came out carrying his glass.

"Why don't you get another one of these," he said, indicating the lounge chair. "They're more comfortable."

The old man put up the back of the chair he had been sleeping in and sat down, and Carl went for the other one and sat in it close to the old man.

"I wonder if Joe's left yet," the old man said.

"I don't think so. He said he'd be late."

"Well, anyway, he'll leave pretty soon. Don't you have to go back to work in two or three weeks?"

"Three. School starts on the eighth and I have to be there a couple of days early."

"I taught writing for years," the old man said, "and I found that sometimes juniors and seniors at Yale were hard to take. I don't know how you manage ninth-graders."

"It's not so bad. I like the kids and they like me." Carl picked up his drink. "But it sure is nice to get out here in the summer."

"Do you ever see any of your students here?"

"My God no. Most of them are only thirteen or fourteen. But sometimes I see one out here a few years after he's been in one of my classes, and that's always a shock."

"I'll bet," the old man said. "Joe was one of my students, you know."

"I know."

The old man put down his glass and looked away, toward the horizon. "He was so young then," he started. "Not like he is now, but really young." The old man went on—

Joe had been a history major at Yale, and sometimes for amusement he had written stories and given them to his friends. His friends liked the stories and flattered Joe and he began to think a little about being a writer, or at least about trying it, and when he began to think about being a writer he decided to try to get into Oswald Stevenson's class.

Mr. Stevenson's class was very popular, and he could not, and did not want to, accommodate everyone who wanted to take it. Instead, he required prospective students to submit a story for his consideration. Many of the stories submitted were fine, accomplished works, and Joe's was not. But most of the fine, accomplished stories were about growing up unhappily or about youthful love or about some sordid aspect of adult life that the young writers could only imperfectly imagine, and Joe's was about reincarnation. He wrote about a soul near the top of the chain of reincarnation, and at the end of the story Joe's character became a glow of light. Much of the story was amateurish, but the final two pages had a warmth and feeling that were rare in the stories submitted to Mr. Stevenson, and Joe was accepted.

Joe's story was one of three stories Mr. Stevenson chose to have read and discussed at the first meeting of the class, and he made copies of the stories for everyone. Joe's story was not the first to be read, and while the first writer read nervously Joe looked impatiently around the room and out the window. When the would-be writer and nervous reader was finished Mr. Stevenson asked for comments, and the comments were polite and filled with phrases like "perhaps you should," or "you might consider," or "it seems," because everyone knew that eventually their work would be subjected to the same attention. Joe was quiet while others spoke, and Mr. Stevenson called on him.

"Well—" he looked at a paper on his desk for a first name, "Joe. What did you think?"

"I thought it was crap," Joe said. He did not seem as though he intended to say any more. The others were quiet, shocked, waiting.

"Could you be more specific?" Mr. Stevenson asked.

"On page one the kid's a perfect child, and then thirteen pages and two hours later he's a total demon. It's just not believable."

Joe sat back and put his hands behind his head.

"And besides that, it's trite. Sure, the language is beautiful, but just because you've got beautiful colors to work with doesn't mean you're going to paint a beautiful picture, or a good picture either."

The young woman who wrote the story laughed nervously and someone coughed, but no one said anything.

60

"Any more comments?" Mr. Stevenson asked, and still no one spoke.

"Well then, why don't you read us yours," he said to Joe.

Joe read his story about reincarnation slowly and sometimes he shut his eyes and spoke from memory. The story ended in a white room filled with low, somber music and then the ceiling dissolved into a starry sky and the room itself, and its contents, dissolved into a dark, formless landscape under the stars, and there was a glow that brightened steadily and rose toward the heavens accompanied by music that swelled and rose with it, and finally the glow became a blaze of light that joined the stars above and the music became an ethereal shimmer of sound.

"Well?" Mr. Stevenson said when Joe was finished reading, "Who's first?"

He looked around the room. No one spoke.

"I'll start then," Mr. Stevenson said, and he told Joe how poor his story was and why it was poor, and the more he talked about Joe's story the less good he had to say about it. Then, when he was finished, the other members of the class had plenty to say about Joe's story, and none of it was very complimentary.

Joe sprawled in his chair and listened, and sometimes he smiled a little. When his eyes met Mr. Stevenson's he smiled. He did not comment after the final story was read and Mr. Stevenson did not call on him.

When the class was over and everyone was picking up their books and leaving Mr. Stevenson came over to Joe's desk.

"Well, did you learn anything today?"

"Yes," Joe said. "People can be petty." He had been preparing to leave, but he stopped and stood up straight. "You know it was a good story."

"No. It was a good idea, but you didn't use it well." Mr. Stevenson was gentler than he had been during class.

61

"Well, I like it."

"And so do I, but I thought you needed to know how that poor girl felt."

Joe did not answer. He picked up his books.

"Would you like some coffee?" Mr. Stevenson asked. "There's a pot by my office."

"Thanks. That would be nice." Joe spoke cautiously.

The two of them walked out together: Joe, a thin young man with long red-brown hair, and Oswald Stevenson, an older man with short hair that was almost entirely gray. They walked across the campus to Mr. Stevenson's office, and as they walked Mr. Stevenson spoke quietly and carefully and Joe spoke with the fervor of a young man who knows he is right. On their way into his office Mr. Stevenson showed Joe where the coffeepot was, down the hall. "I've got some cups in my office," he said.

Mr. Stevenson's office was littered with books and papers. The top of his desk was covered with stacks of papers that had slid over each other, and books lay scattered about facedown, open. Books were jammed into bookcases and were piled in front of them.

"Christ," Joe said to himself.

Mr. Stevenson did not hear.

"There are the cups." He pointed to two filthy cups sitting on a pile of books.

"Christ," Joe said again.

"Why don't you get some coffee while I straighten up a little," Mr. Stevenson said.

Joe agreed, and before he poured the coffee he went into the men's room and washed the cups. When he came back Mr. Stevenson was moving piles of papers.

"I'm sorry about this mess." He gestured around the room. "I don't work here, I work at home, and where I work has to be very neat. So I bring everything here that I don't know where to put at home."

62

Joe said, "Oh."

"Besides, the woman who takes care of my house would throw it all out if I left it at home."

Joe thought that would be wise but he did not say so. Instead, he gave Mr. Stevenson a cup of coffee and sat down in an old green armchair.

"You know," Mr. Stevenson said. "Your problem with writing is that you don't know something Gertrude Stein wrote. She wrote that she wrote for herself and strangers. You've got to remember the strangers."

"It's hard to know how a stranger will read something you've written," Joe answered.

"Of course. As you read your own work you not only remember what you wrote but you remember what you were thinking about when you wrote it. Your own writing becomes a kind of shorthand that calls up the ideas you had when you wrote it. But you've got to realize that those ideas are yours alone; the reader will never know them—"

—Even then the old man had tended to run on a bit when he spoke, and now, as he sat with Carl on his deck in the warm afternoon sun, he remembered and spoke freely. The old man seldom spoke about himself or about his past or about Joe's past and Carl gently encouraged him to continue—

Joe, that afternoon in Mr. Stevenson's office, had asked Mr. Stevenson if he had written things he considered failures.

"God yes." Mr. Stevenson laughed. "My failures would fill one of those filing cabinets." He waved toward the wall.

"Anything recently?"

Mr. Stevenson did not usually talk about his own work with students, but this time he did.

"Yes, last spring," he answered. "Do you remember that car accident a year ago that killed the two seniors in one car and the two high school students in the other?"

"Yes. I knew one of the guys a little."

"So how did you feel when you heard about the accident?"

"I don't know. Shocked I guess."

"Well, I tried to write about that. I tried to write about two people who had every expectation of continuing to live and were suddenly killed. I tried to write about the people who knew them, and about the seemingly innocent chain of events that led to their deaths, but it just didn't work. When I first wrote it, it seemed as if I killed the characters off suddenly just to finish the book, so then I put the accident first and that didn't work either; then the rest of it seemed, to use your word, trite, and anticlimactic. But you know, most lives, even the lives of extraordinary people, are very trite most of the time."

Mr. Stevenson and Joe continued to talk about Mr. Stevenson's failed book and Joe gradually began to feel as though it was an ordinary thing to be talking with an author of Mr. Stevenson's reputation about why one of the author's books had failed. They talked and the coffee grew cold in their cups and the afternoon passed on, and then Mr. Stevenson noticed the length of the shadows outside.

"I'm sorry," Mr. Stevenson said, "I've got to go. I'm driving down to New York this afternoon."

"Do you go down often?" Joe asked as he stood up.

"Not as often as I should. I've got an apartment there, and I almost never use it."

"Will you be there through the weekend?"

"Yes. I'm coming back Sunday afternoon." Mr. Stevenson was picking up papers and stuffing them into his briefcase.

"I'm going to be in the city this weekend too. Maybe we could meet for a drink," Joe said.

Mr. Stevenson did not answer for a minute. He rarely socialized with students, and he had never invited a student to his house in New Haven or his apartment in New York.

64

"I guess that would be all right," he said slowly. "How about Saturday?"

They agreed on a time and Mr. Stevenson gave Joe his telephone number, which was unlisted, and they agreed that Joe would come to Mr. Stevenson's apartment. Mr. Stevenson motioned for Joe to precede him out of his office and he looked at Joe's long hair.

"I don't understand why students wear their hair so long," he said—

—The bell by the gate rang loudly and startled the old man out of his memories, and he stopped his monologue.

"Would you see who that is," he asked Carl.

"It's probably Lonny."

Carl got up and went around the house. When he came back he had Lonny with him.

"Hi," Lonny said. "Carl tells me you've been telling him about Joe."

"I guess I have," the old man said, "I guess I have."

"Would you like a drink?" the old man asked.

"Sure."

"Let's all have one," the old man said, and he stood up and led them through the house into the kitchen.

"Wine for me," he said, opening the refrigerator. "Could you get out some glasses, Carl?"

"Could I have a G and T?" Lonny asked.

"Here's the tonic." The old man handed Lonny a cold bottle from the refrigerator. "And a lime." He handed out a lime and reached back for a bottle of Sancerre. While the old man opened the bottle of wine and poured some for himself, Lonny cut two wedges from the lime and Carl made the gin and tonics. The old man put the wine bottle back in the refrigerator and they went back out onto the deck.

"Why don't you two sit on the lounge chairs," the old man said.

65

"No thanks," Lonny answered. "I like this better." He pulled over a canvas chair and the old man and Carl sat in the lounge chairs as they had before Lonny arrived.

"So," Lonny asked, "how'd you meet him?"

"Well," the old man replied, "he was in one of my classes. But then he met me in New York too." The old man drifted back into his memories easily, encouraged by the gentle wash of the waves and the warmth of the sun and the expansiveness of the sea—

Joe had arrived at Mr. Stevenson's apartment exactly on time, and when Mr. Stevenson opened the door neither of them knew what to say.

"Come in," Mr. Stevenson said, and Joe came in. He stood in the entryway and put his hands under his blazer into the pockets of his jeans.

"This is a nice place," and "Do you want a drink?" they said simultaneously, and Joe said why didn't they go out and Mr. Stevenson said that he might as well take the grand tour as long as he was there, and he showed Joe his apartment. Unlike his office, his apartment was neat and austerely furnished. The books were ordered and the kitchen looked new and unused. "Do you cook here?" Joe asked.

"Almost never," Mr. Stevenson called from the bedroom where he was getting a jacket.

Joe opened the refrigerator. In it was a bottle of orange juice and a can of coffee, as well as a couple of bottles of soda and tonic water.

"I guess you don't."

Mr. Stevenson came into the kitchen and they shut off the lights and left. It was one of those days in early September that are as hot as midsummer and only the angle and length of the shadows shows that it is not. They walked down the street toward Fifth Avenue and Joe admired some of the young men

66

who were out enjoying the early evening hours, and he noticed that Mr. Stevenson was admiring them too.

"Have you ever walked through the park?" Joe asked.

"Not in years."

"Then let's cut across the end."

"Do you know where you're going?" Mr. Stevenson asked.

"Of course," Joe said, although he was not certain.

They went into the park and followed a path that led to a foot bridge at the end of a small lake. From the bridge they could see the buildings along Fifth Avenue and Central Park South turning golden in the light of the setting sun. From the park they walked to a café and sat at a table on the sidewalk. They talked about what they would drink, and they talked about Yale, and then their wine came, and gradually they began to talk more easily and they began to talk about writing and they began to talk about famous writers. Mr. Stevenson did not like to talk about himself, but he was comfortable talking about other writers.

"I met Gertrude Stein once, twice in fact," he said.

"When?" Joe asked.

"The first time was in 1934. Of course I was a child then."

"Of course," Joe said.

"She and Miss Toklas were staying at the Algonquin and someone I knew whom she knew took me to meet her."

"Who was that?" Joe asked, and Mr. Stevenson told him about an older man who had not had much to do in the twenties and thirties except have outrageous affairs with men and women on both sides of the Atlantic, but who could talk intelligently about almost anything except the works of Shakespeare, which he claimed put him in a stupor after a few lines.

"What'd you and Miss Stein talk about?"

"Food," Mr. Stevenson said. "She talked about American

67

food and how good it was and how moist it was. I wanted to talk about writing but she said to come to one of her lectures. My friend wanted her to offer him a drink but she didn't, and after we left he said she was an old bitch."

"Was she?"

"No. Humility wasn't one of her attributes, but she had reason to be proud of her work."

"God, why?" Joe asked. "She couldn't even write English."

Mr. Stevenson was very fond of the writings of Gertrude Stein and he defended her strongly.

"That's not true," he said. "When you read her work for the first time you really have to work to read it, and when you finish you're sometimes not sure exactly what you have read, but you usually know it is something worthwhile and not just nonsense. Parts of *Making of Americans* are like that. Although it is not a success as a novel, parts of it are worth reading. The first time you read the repetitive parts it is maddening and you think you might not finish and you put it down, but then it bothers you and you pick it up again and use a pencil to keep track of the weaving and reweaving of the same words into different sentences and finally you finish. And when you do you have learned something about writing and thinking and talking, and you have learned it as much by the way she wrote as by what she wrote."

Mr. Stevenson stopped, and for the first time he smiled openly at Joe. "I guess I do run on a bit," he said. "It's one of the side effects of being old and living alone."

"You're not that old," Joe said.

"Old enough."

"Well, you're not going to get any younger so you might as well not worry about it."

Mr. Stevenson took pride in how fit he was for his age and in how young he looked.

"I suppose I'm not getting any younger, but sometimes I think age is better than the brashness of youth," he said coldly.

"Being neither brash nor old, I wouldn't know," Joe said.

Mr. Stevenson laughed. "You're something," he said, and Joe smiled.

"Anyway," Joe said, "you're wrong about Gertrude Stein. Some of her stuff doesn't mean anything."

"Maybe it doesn't. But in some things there is no intellectual content intended; only the form is important."

"Huh?"

"When you destroyed that poor girl's ego in front of the class you talked about painting. Well, as painters sometimes rearrange elements of a landscape or a still life or even a portrait into a different composition, so she rearranged sentences into new sentences that didn't necessarily mean anything. Then too, as painters sometimes made compositions that weren't formed from parts of something else but were just color and lines and shapes, or sometimes just color, Gertrude sometimes just wrote pure compositions; she didn't rearrange sentences that were originally sensible, she joined words in ways that pleased her and that robbed them of their usual meaning."

Joe looked as though he had stopped listening and Mr. Stevenson noticed it.

"Sorry," he said. "Once you get a writer started about writing it's hard to stop him."

"I think it's interesting. You're interesting."

"It's an attribute of the advanced age you seem to think I have," Mr. Stevenson said with a smile.

Both of their glasses were empty. "More wine?" Mr. Stevenson asked.

"Sure. That would be nice."

Mr. Stevenson motioned to a waiter, who nodded and went inside, and Mr. Stevenson and Joe watched a shirtless young man trying to run past. The sidewalk was very crowded and the frustrated young man finally stopped running and walked. He looked at his watch exasperatedly.

"Handsome guy," Joe said.

Mr. Stevenson did not answer, but he looked at the runner and then looked carefully at Joe.

"I've done all of the talking so far," he said. "Tell me something about you."

"I wouldn't say that lecturing about Gertrude Stein was telling me about yourself."

Mr. Stevenson laughed. "All right, tell me about something you think about."

The waiter came with two more glasses of wine and they both thanked him.

"History," Joe said.

"That's pretty broad," Mr. Stevenson commented.

"Well, I guess the part of history I like best is studying how individual men made significant changes in history."

"No women?"

"I guess there were a few like Elizabeth the First and maybe Joan of Arc, but I don't know much about them. I'm more interested in men like Caesar and Napoleon and Alexander the Great and Hitler."

Mr. Stevenson had been thinking about the young man across the table from him and not listening carefully to what he was saying, but now he concentrated on the conversation again.

"You surely don't think that Hitler was in the same company as the others, do you? At least the others are thought by historians to have done some good, although I'm not sure I'd agree with them about Alexander."

"I don't know much about writing," Joe said, "but I know that it's hard to assess the worth of something you write until after you've put it away for a while and forgotten it.

Then when you look at it again you have an idea about whether it's good. Don't you agree?"

Mr. Stevenson nodded. "Certainly, but that doesn't have anything to do with Hitler."

"Yes it does," Joe said. "Where in writing it may take a writer a month or two, or even a year or two, to decide if something is good, in history it takes the world centuries to judge the positive or negative effects of an event or a man."

"I hope you're not going to tell me that Hitler provided any benefit to the world."

"Hitler was the very personification of insanity and evil," Joe said. "But we won't know the ultimate effects of his actions in your lifetime or even mine. Who knows what is going to result from the partitioning of Europe into Soviet and American spheres of influence? Or Israel? Look at what she's done in the last two wars. In a century or so Israel might be a major world power. Now there's Russia, China, and the United States. God knows Europe will never unite, but maybe if the U.S. can keep Russia at bay Israel will become the fourth major power by overrunning the Middle East."

Mr. Stevenson was beginning to think that Joe was a more serious young man than he had thought when he had first met him. "What about Vietnam?" he asked.

"An insignificant speck in the galaxy of world history." Joe laughed. "Unless, of course, I get drafted and get my head shot off. Or worse."

"You know a lot for your age," Mr. Stevenson said.

"I know," Joe replied. He smiled straight at Mr. Stevenson.

Mr. Stevenson swirled his wineglass on the table. "Tell me," he said, "do you know the meaning of the word humility?"

"Isn't that a disease Christians have?"

Mr. Stevenson laughed. "You certainly are a bright young man."

"Right again," Joe said.

Mr. Stevenson was watching the people on the sidewalk. "Now that's funny," he said. He indicated an obese bag lady. She was dressed in several layers of tattered clothes and she had a large nest of shopping bags in each hand. When she walked she lurched one leg forward, then the other, and she swayed from side to side and her shoulders jerked up and down as she progressed. She walked close to their table and a sharp, unwashed smell came to them.

"Funny," Joe said. "You have a sick sense of humor."

"Not funny like that. Look at her size. She must take in thousands of calories of food a day to maintain that weight, and I always thought the street people were street people because they were broke. Those thousands of calories must cost quite a bit of money."

"Maybe she eats children."

"Now who has the sick sense of humor?" Mr. Stevenson asked.

Their glasses were both empty again and Mr. Stevenson asked Joe if he wanted more and Joe said no.

"But how about dinner?" he asked.

"I'm sorry, but I'm meeting an old friend," Mr. Stevenson told him.

"But you said I knew a lot for my age," Joe answered, and Mr. Stevenson laughed.

"Yes, I guess you do, and my old friend is boring anyway."

"Well?"

"All right," Mr. Stevenson said. "I've got to make a call then." He left the table, and when he was away Joe asked the waiter for the check and paid it, and then he sat and watched the people stream by.

"It's settled," Mr. Stevenson said when he came back.

"May I have the check, please," he said to the waiter as he passed.

"It's already been paid," the waiter told him. He nodded at Joe.

"You shouldn't have done that," Mr. Stevenson said. "But thank you. Dinner's on me. Where would you like to go?"

Joe told him about a place in the Village. Mr. Stevenson seldom went down to the Village and he was seldom in the company of someone forty years younger, so he was not completely comfortable with the suggestion. But he agreed, and they stood up to leave.

"Can you make it walking?" Joe asked.

Mr. Stevenson prided himself on his fitness and he was annoyed.

"Can you?" he asked, and the two of them started down Sixth Avenue walking rapidly. Soon Mr. Stevenson noticed with satisfaction that Joe was perspiring.

"Too much for you?" he said.

"Listen," Joe told him, "if we're racing just let me know and I'm going to run."

Mr. Stevenson did not reply, but he slowed down. For a few minutes it was not pleasant between them.

"Christ, you're an old fool," Mr. Stevenson said to himself.

"What was that?" Joe turned toward him.

"Nothing. Talking to myself," Mr. Stevenson said, and they walked on. In the west, down the streets and between the rows of buildings, they could see the sunset. It had a perfection usually found only in the imagination, or in dreams. At the horizon the sky was orange, higher it faded to pink and then to blue. High up, but not overhead, a single small cloud hung, dark purple underneath and almost black on top. Above them the sky was a deep crystalline blue that darkened as they walked.

"Such sights make life worthwhile," Mr. Stevenson said. Joe did not answer immediately and when he did it was not exactly a response to his companion's statement.

"You remember that story I read in class?" he asked.

"It was only this week," Mr. Stevenson said. "As you said, I won't get any younger, but I'm not senile."

He was joking, but Joe ignored it. "If I get sent to Vietnam, and if I get killed, I don't want to have a funeral. I just want to have that story read to whomever will listen."

"You know, the old friend I disappointed tonight is boring, but he is not maudlin," Mr. Stevenson said.

"I'm sorry. I was just thinking."

They were in Chelsea now, and they passed a dingy-looking shop that had a sign over the door announcing that fortunes were read. They looked inside, cupping their hands against the glass to see more clearly. A curtain divided the old store into a front and back room, and the trappings of gypsy fortune-telling were everywhere. While they stood there a woman, obviously the visionary the sign referred to, came up from behind them. She looked a little like Carmen from the opera of the same name; she had a full, red skirt, huge earrings, jangling jewelry, and long black hair. Mr. Stevenson and Joe each thought unkind thoughts as they watched her knock on the door. Then the curtain at the back of the front room was pushed aside by a small black-haired boy who ran to the door and unlocked it and leaped happily into his mother's arms. She hugged him and they disappeared inside, chattering happily in a language that neither Joe nor Mr. Stevenson understood.

They smiled at each other and walked on. "I think Gertrude Stein was right," Mr. Stevenson said. "She thought that all of the different people in the world could be sorted into a finite number of types and that those types could all be described. She said that was what she was doing in part of *The Making of Americans*."

"Are you going to start lecturing again?"

Mr. Stevenson was quiet, and Joe could see that he had been offended.

"Hey," he said, "I was kidding. You've made me interested enough to actually want to read some of her stuff."

"I hope it won't be a strain," Mr. Stevenson said sourly. Then he laughed. "I don't think it will be."

They passed a reeking man who was sleeping on a grate in the sidewalk, and as they passed a train rumbled below and a blast of hot air shot up through the grate. The man did not move. An empty bottle was by his head and he smelled of urine.

"I think there's one Gertrude missed," Mr. Stevenson said.

They walked on and they looked at the sky in the west and they each thought about the other and about Gertrude Stein.

"You said you met Miss Stein twice. When was the second time?" Joe asked.

"Oh, it was a year or so later in Paris. It was in the fall. She talked about money and she said that money was funny and she said she had written about is money money or is money not money."

"I don't think that's very clear to me," Joe said.

"Me either." Mr. Stevenson laughed again. "But it seemed clear to her, and she certainly did want people to know that she had money."

"She was in France during the war, wasn't she?"

"Both wars."

"What did she think about Hitler?"

"Well, in the early thirties she wrote about him as Father Hitler. She also wrote about Stalin as Father Stalin, and there were some other fathers I don't remember. But she also observed herself that she was mostly wrong about politics, and later she became quite bitter about Hitler."

75

"You know, I wrote a paper about Hitler's use of propaganda for a history course last year."

"No, I didn't know."

"It's just an expression," Joe said.

"Yes, but what does it mean?"

"For Christ's sake," Joe said. "I don't know. It's just a way to get the motor running. You've used it a few times tonight yourself. But anyway, listen. For this paper I found a great quote from one of Hitler's speeches. He said that Churchill had been chasing around Europe like a madman looking for something to set on fire, and that Churchill was finding hirelings who opened the gates of their countries to him. Can you believe that Hitler said that about Churchill?"

"I wonder if Hitler believed himself?"

"If he did he was mad, and he was mad so he did."

"There's something wrong with that reasoning."

"Well, you get the idea," Joe said. "Anyway, we're here." They were in front of a brownstone in the west part of Greenwich Village. There were pots of flowers along an iron fence that ran in front of the building, and pots of flowers lined the short flight of steps that led down to the restaurant from the street. They walked down and in and the young man who seated them said hi to Joe as if he knew him and he said good evening to Mr. Stevenson, and he tried to decide if he knew who Mr. Stevenson was. He gave them a table by the windows and they looked up at the street. They ordered wine.

Mr. Stevenson looked around the room and he noticed that most of the tables were occupied by young men.

"Do you come here often?" he asked.

"When I'm in the city," Joe said. Since he did not say how often he was in the city it was not a complete answer to the question.

They had a pleasant meal. They talked about Gertrude Stein and about writing, and they talked about Nixon and Vietnam and Israel, and they lingered and did not want the meal to be over. When they were finally without a doubt finished and the check had come and Mr. Stevenson had paid it, neither of them wanted to end their conversation. However, they were the last customers in the restaurant and around them the waiters were cleaning and straightening and preparing for the next day.

"I guess it's time to go," Joe said.

"I guess it is," Mr. Stevenson said, and they stood and walked toward the door.

The young man who had seated them came over to say good-bye. "May I ask if you're Oswald Stevenson?" he said.

"I think you just did. Yes, I am."

"I hope you enjoyed everything," the young man said. "We'd like to see you again."

"I'm not even sure I could find it without my brash young friend here."

"That's OK. You can bring him too," the young man said, and everyone laughed and they moved to the door.

"Are you going to be out later?" the young man asked Joe.

"I don't know," Joe said. "If I am, you know where I'll be."

They all said good-bye and Joe and Mr. Stevenson walked out and up the steps and into the night. It had grown cooler while they had been in the restaurant but it was not cold. As they stood on the sidewalk deciding what to do, an unshaven man wearing frayed evening clothes asked them in accented English if they could spare some change. He sounded like Maurice Chevalier. Mr. Stevenson waved him away, but Joe stopped and searched through his pockets and when he could only find seventeen cents he took out his wallet and handed the man a dollar.

"I liked the accent," he told Mr. Stevenson.

"It's your money," Mr. Stevenson said, and then he said, "I want to thank you for a nice evening."

"The pleasure was yours."

"Are you always like that?" Mr. Stevenson asked.

"Sometimes. Come on, let's walk a little," Joe said, and the two of them walked down to Sheridan Square and across to Fifth Avenue and on to University Place.

"I'm going to catch a cab," Mr. Stevenson said.

"May I share it with you?" Joe asked. "I'm going uptown too."

Mr. Stevenson said of course, and they hailed a cab and got in.

"Uptown please," Mr. Stevenson told the driver.

"Where may I drop you?" he asked Joe.

"I'm coming with you," Joe told him.

"I'm sorry, but I'm tired and I've really had enough to drink and the only place I'm going is to bed."

The taxi was speeding uptown as they spoke and they were jostled from side to side.

"I know," Joe said. "Wouldn't you like company?"

Mr. Stevenson thought that Joe was interested in him because of who he was, and he was angered. It had happened before with opportunistic young men who thought of themselves as great but undiscovered writers.

"You can do anything you want," he said coldly. "If you need a place to stay I'll give you money for a hotel."

"You don't have to be mean," Joe said quietly, and Mr. Stevenson saw and heard that Joe was serious and again he thought that Joe's demeanor might conceal a different personality than he had assumed. He sighed.

"I'm an old man," he said.

"I know. July fourth, 1911. I did my homework." Joe smiled but Mr. Stevenson did not see it in the darkness in the back of the cab.

"I guess you did," Mr. Stevenson said.

"Did you know that on that Fourth of July there was a

78

nationwide heat wave and all over the country people died in the heat? Twenty-eight in New York alone."

"Do you have any more surprises?" Mr. Stevenson asked.

"Maybe. But don't you want to hear more about the day you were born?"

"By all means." Mr. Stevenson did not feel in control of the situation.

And Joe told him about the day he was born. Twenty-eight persons were drowned in the New York Metropolitan area; Atwood flew from New York to Atlantic City in five hours with only three stops and upon his arrival received a tumultuous welcome and a trophy from *The New York Times;* a balloonist was lost over Lake Michigan; there was a fire in a Michigan prison for the criminally insane; it was 100 degrees Fahrenheit in Cincinnati; the suffragettes paraded down Fifth Avenue in stagecoaches.

"I got the date from *Who's Who,*" Joe said, "and I looked up the papers for the day at New York Public this morning."

"You mean you planned this?"

"I was a boy scout."

"I don't know why I don't see the relevance of that," Mr. Stevenson said.

"You know, be prepared."

"Oh," Mr. Stevenson said.

The next morning Mr. Stevenson was up and had showered, dressed, and made coffee while Joe still slept. Finally, when he was taking some things from a drawer and putting them into a canvas bag, Joe opened his eyes.

"God, what time is it?" he said. His voice was thick.

"It's almost nine." Mr. Stevenson was looking through drawers for something he could not seem to find.

Joe rolled over and put his head in the pillow. "God," he said. It sounded like *grd.*

Mr. Stevenson found what he was looking for and put it into his bag.

"I'm going swimming," he said. "Do you want to come?"

"Swimming? Swimming! My God, it's nine o'clock in the morning."

"I know," Mr. Stevenson said. "I'm late."

"Where in hell do you swim at nine o'clock on Sunday morning?"

"At a club. I swim every day I can, either here or back at school. In the summers I swim in the ocean."

"I don't have any trunks, thank God," Joe said.

"That's all right. I've got extras, and they have them at the club." Mr. Stevenson went into the bathroom and Joe could see him brushing his teeth.

"Christ," Joe said to himself. He got up, naked, and leaned against the bathroom door. "Do you believe in coffee first, or is the shock part of the fun?"

Joe got himself a mug of coffee and showered and dressed and complained and within thirty minutes he was ready to go.

It was a long pool and Mr. Stevenson swam slow easy laps with slow effortless turns at each end and Joe splashed along beside him for as long as he could, which was not long. Then, while Mr. Stevenson continued to swim his slow easy laps and make his slow effortless turns, Joe sat on the edge of the pool with his feet in the water. At first his chest heaved and he could feel his heart in his temples. As the heaving stopped and the pounding stopped he began to feel completely enervated and he thought about a comfortable bed with clean white sheets, and still Mr. Stevenson swam. Finally he was finished and he climbed out of the pool and pulled Joe up and they walked to the locker room.

"That's pretty good for an old man," Joe said.

"Do you have to call me that?" the old man who had just swum a mile with slow clean easy strokes said.

"It's that or Oswald," Joe told him, and Joe began to call him Old Man—

The tide was coming in as the old man talked, and the waves no longer teased at the shore but fell onto it with a good weight. They had all finished their drinks and when the old man noticed he stopped talking and remembering and looked away from the sea.

"I guess I do rattle on," he said.

"Rattle on? You should write it down," Lonny said. "It's beautiful."

"Writing has to be more than beautiful," the old man told him. "Besides, it's too personal.

"Do you guys want another drink?" he asked.

They both said yes and they went inside to make their drinks and pour some wine for the old man, and he sat and watched and listened to the gulls and he wondered exactly where Joe was and what he was doing, and he thought a little, but not too much, about what living would be like without Joe, and he thought about how lucky he was. It did not occur to him to think about how lucky Joe was, but everyone who knew the old man and Joe thought that Joe was lucky too.

Carl and Lonny came back to the deck and Carl said that he had to leave after that drink and that it had to be a quick one. "I don't," Lonny said, and the old man smiled and said that Lonny could stay as long as he wanted.

"If Joe couldn't swim very well back then, why does he swim so well now?" Carl asked.

"Well," the old man said, "that fall he rented a room in my house—" He broke off. "Actually that's another story, but he did and he made me take money for it. Anyway, when he moved in, which was in October I think, he began swimming every day with me, and you know how Joe doesn't like to do anything poorly."

Carl nodded.

"Well, then he began swimming on his own too, and the next summer, that was his first summer out here with me, he swam twice a day, up to Sailors' Haven and back, and by the end of that summer I couldn't keep up with him."

"I remember that summer," Carl said. "That was my first summer out here too. I remember lying on the beach in the beginning of the summer and seeing someone swimming up and down the beach and thinking there goes that guy who lives with the old guy."

Carl looked at the old man. "Sorry," he said. "I didn't know either of you then. I didn't get to know you until you, really Joe I guess, began to have those parties that half of the island showed up for."

"I am an old guy," the old man said. "But it's better than the alternative." He thought about that summer, now ten summers ago. "I didn't get any work done that summer, but those parties were fun." He turned toward Lonny. "Joe was a little younger than you are, I think, and that was when I learned how young I wasn't. I tried to keep up with Joe for a while, and I've never been so tired in my life."

Carl started to speak, but the old man was looking out to sea again and Carl stopped.

"I'll never forget that Joe looked up *The New York Times* for the day I was born," the old man started. "A few years ago, when I was still at Yale and Joe was a grad student there, I went to an estate sale out in the country someplace. An old woman had died who had never thrown anything out, and all of *The New York Times* from back to the forties were piled in neat piles in her attic. I asked the people running the sale if I could buy some of the papers and they said I could have all of them for twenty-five dollars. I found a few that had some historical importance, but I also found the papers from the day Joe was born and the day after, and I gave them to him. We still have them back in New York."

"Anything interesting happen?" Lonny asked.

"Not really. Harold Ross, the founder and editor of *The New Yorker,* died. I can remember reading about it back then, and if anyone had told me that out in Illinois a boy was being born with the same last name who would change my life I wouldn't have believed it. I still think about it: about all of the forks in all of the roads of each of our histories and how each of us many, many times had to take the right path so we would both come to Yale and then so he would be in my class, and then . . ."

He stopped and smiled. "I guess you know the rest."

"The rest, as they say, is history," Lonny said, raising his glass.

"Yes, but it's more than that," the old man said reflectively. "It's almost like fate. Not the god-determined fate of the Greeks, but the fact that many times in life we make decisions that will make our lives go one way or another, and once the decision is made there is no going back. Of course, you can change your mind about something, but even then your life might not be the same as it would have been if you hadn't made the decision you changed your mind about. Sometime I'd like to start a book, write fifty pages or so, and construct a decision point for a character—something trivial like, perhaps like whether to go to a store or not—and then write two completely different books after that point, one for each decision."

"You lost me," Lonny said. "Were you speaking English?"

Carl and the old man laughed, and then Lonny laughed also.

"That would be complicated if there were more than two alternatives," Carl said.

"It sure would," the old man agreed, "but I'm thinking about doing it for just two." The old man had forgotten that the day before he had said that he might not write another book.

"It must be after four, and I know you have to work early tonight," the old man said to Carl.

"Yes, and I've got to go," Carl said. "But I've really enjoyed listening to you."

"You're too kind to an old man who talks too much," the old man said as the three of them stood up.

"Oh, stay out here," Carl told him. "I can find the door."

"All right, we will," the old man answered, and Carl told Lonny he'd see him later and said good-bye to the old man and he went through the house and left his glass in the kitchen, and he went out across the deck and out through the gate.

The old man and Lonny drank wine and gin and tonic and talked about Lonny and Joe and dancing and Fire Island but not about writing. While they talked Bob came down the beach on his dune bike. He did not stop, but he waved to them and they waved back.

"What's he do in the winter?" Lonny asked.

"Well," the old man said, "there are some policemen out here in the winter, but Bob isn't one of them. He spends the winter on the force over in Port Jefferson."

"You know, this is a beautiful house," Lonny said.

"It wouldn't be much without the sea."

"Oh, I don't know. If you got in a bunch of big plants and some of those rattan chairs with the big round backs it'd be nice anywhere."

The old man did not respond. He was watching the sea.

"Did you ever think of getting some of those kind of chairs?" Lonny asked.

"Not really." The old man did not look away from the sea.

"You should, you know."

"I'll talk to Joe about it," the old man said. He would talk to Joe about it, and he thought about what Joe would say and he laughed a little.

"What's funny?" Lonny asked.

84

"Joe. He makes me laugh sometimes. Yesterday he reminded me of an otter."

"He doesn't have fur," Lonny said.

"I know, but he plays in the water like an otter does."

"He reminds me of an angel."

The old man looked away from the sea and over at Lonny, who had taken off his shirt and arranged himself so that the sun was hitting him directly in the face and chest.

"An angel?"

"You know how he's so quiet and calm, and he has that little smile that makes you want to smile when you see him?"

"Yes. He makes me smile too."

"Well, that's what I think an angel would be like. Quiet and smiling."

The old man thought about Lonny's comment about fur and he smiled. "What about feathers?"

"The angels I think about are men. They do not have feathers," Lonny said firmly.

"What makes you think about angels at all?"

Lonny crossed his legs on the chair and looked at the old man.

"When I was little someone sent me a postcard of a painting of an angel. I lost it a long time ago, but I can still remember it. The angel was a man with a long robe. It was blue, almost turquoise. He was leading a boy by the hand, and he looked down at the boy with the sweetest smile. I wished I could find an angel like that. Still do, I guess."

The old man tried to remember the orders of angels. Was it seraphim, cherubim, wheels, dominions, virtues, powers, principalities, archangels, and angels? The old man decided that it was and he was pleased with himself for remembering.

"Joe went to a party out here once dressed as an angel," the old man said.

"Ya?"

"He sure did. At first he wanted to go as Azrael, the angel

85

of death. Azrael is covered with a thousand veils so that only God can see him, and his body is covered with billions of eyes. Whenever an eye closes, someone dies. Joe was going to paint eyes all over himself and then wear a floor-length transparent veil."

"That," Lonny said, "is weird."

"Oh, he didn't do it. He just went as an ordinary angel all in white. He made wings from wire and paper and he covered them with rows and rows of real feathers. It took him a month to make them."

"I'll bet," Lonny said.

"We were quite a pair. I put on a long beard and went as God—" The old man drifted off, smiling at the memory of the befeathered and besequined and painted and half-naked partygoers sweeping through the Grove in the late afternoon, before the party, so that their costumes could be admired by as many people as possible.

After that neither of them had much to say. The old man looked out to sea and thought about angels and Joe and parties that he and Joe had attended, and Lonny sat to the sun and thought about angels and Joe, but differently. They each sat and thought their thoughts, and gradually the old man came back from the sea and noticed that Lonny's glass was empty.

"Would you like another gin and tonic?" the old man asked.

Lonny turned back and looked at the old man and said, "No thanks, I should go," and the old man did not try to stop him but he was glad that Lonny had come. They stood up and the old man said that he thought he might rest a little before Joe came back, and they walked through the house and into the kitchen with their glasses and the old man noticed that it was five o'clock. He thanked Lonny for coming.

"Would you like to have dinner at the restaurant with Joe and me later?" he asked.

"Sure," Lonny answered.

"We'll do it then. Should we stop over at Carl's house for you?"

"I think I'm going to change and go down to the restaurant to see Carl, so why don't you meet me there?"

"It might be as late as nine."

"That's OK. I'll be there," Lonny said, and he said good-bye and the old man said good-bye, and Lonny walked across the deck and out the gate as the old man watched from the door. Lonny gave the bell a good ring.

The old man was tired, both from the champagne the night before and the wine that afternoon, and he climbed to the loft and lay down. The windows were all open. He could see the sea and a breeze blew across him, and the breeze and the sound of the waves lulled him into a tranquil sleep.

He dreamed of angels. A double line of angels came walking toward him from the sea; they walked on the waves and the sun hit their robes, which were brightly white and billowed around them without getting wet. When the angels reached the shore they milled about in a group, and then there was a gap in the old man's dream, and then he dreamed about gulls scrambling and flapping and squawking to reach a bit of food that had been found on the beach, and then the gulls flew up in a flock and swept around and headed out to sea and as they flew away they grew larger and whiter and again the old man dreamed of angels.

After Lonny left he went to Carl's house to change for the evening. It was warm and he changed into fresh shorts and a tight shirt. He tried on several combinations before he found one that satisfied him, and when he was satisfied he spent some time looking at himself in the mirror. He stretched and turned, trying to see his back and his profile, and he looked carefully at his face and then he was ready to go.

When he arrived at the restaurant the disco was blasting in the front room, and he went into the disco first instead of the restaurant. He spoke to people he knew, said hello to Sherwood, the friendliest bartender east of San Francisco, danced a little, and thought about whether he would take any drugs but decided not to. When he was ready to go in to see Carl he said good-bye to everyone in the disco he knew, although he was only going to the next room. He walked in and saw Robert busy at his stand-up desk. He stopped for Robert to admire him.

"Hey, how're you?" Robert said.

"Dry," Lonny answered. Carl could see him from the inside bar where he was working and Lonny waved. "I was over at Joe's. Boy, the old man sure talks a lot."

"So do you," Robert said, "and you aren't even old."

"Some of us never get old, honey."

Robert turned to a customer and Lonny drifted into the bar. He took a seat by a man who looked alone.

"Hi, I'm Lonny," he said, and the man turned toward him and smiled and told him his name. Carl came over.

"How'd you and the old man get along?"

"Good. He talked and I listened."

"What was he doing when you left?"

"He said he was going to take a nap," Lonny said. "What's a fella got to do to get a drink around here, anyway?" Lonny smiled at the man next to him.

"Give my friend a drink," the man said, and Carl introduced Lonny and the man and Carl brought Lonny a gin and tonic. Carl went to wait on another customer and Lonny and the man talked and eventually the man bought Lonny another gin and tonic and Lonny said thank you and that he wanted to walk around a bit, and he got up, took his drink, and wandered out into the disco.

"He's some kid," the man at the bar said to Carl. Carl was wiping the bar where Lonny's drink had been.

"I don't think that *kid* is exactly the right word," Carl said. He looked toward the entrance and saw Bob, the

88

policeman, come in, and he waved. Bob walked quickly to where Robert was standing and did not wave back. Carl shrugged and turned to a customer who wanted his attention.

Robert and Bob came into the bar and Robert motioned to Carl.

"Hi, Bob," Carl said as he came over to them.

"Joe's had an accident," Robert said.

Carl stopped smiling.

"Where?"

"Up on the Sunrise Highway," Bob said. "His car was hit by a van that cut a light. It came over the police radio. He was carrying a card that said to notify Mr. Stevenson if there was an emergency, and they don't have a telephone out here."

Carl asked the question and as he asked it his heart started to accelerate as he thought of the possible answers.

"How is he?"

"DOA," Bob said.

Carl took a step back.

"Oh Christ. Oh bloody fucking Jesus Christ!"

As he spoke his mind reached for a frame of reference and searched for an area of stability from which to work. Anxiety, surprise, fear, helplessness, and anger whirled through him in confusion. Then he remembered, suddenly and vividly, swimming with Joe the day before and how brown and hard Joe had looked and how easily he had played in the water, and a wave of heat washed over Carl and he felt his face and neck grow warm and he began to sweat.

"GOD DAMN IT!" he said. He clenched his hands into fists and put them one on top of the other on the bar and rested his forehead on them and rocked back and forth on his feet.

Bob stood back and did not speak. Robert held the end of his strand of beads tightly.

"Carl, listen," Robert said. "The old man doesn't know yet."

89

Carl looked at Bob. "What do you mean he doesn't know? Isn't that your job?" Carl said to him. He ducked under the bar and stood in front of it. The attention of the customers was attracted and some thought that the old man had been in an accident and some thought that Joe had been in an accident and everyone there gradually was watching and wondering, but no one asked.

"Carl, Carl." Robert put his arm around Carl's shoulders and pulled him away from the bar. "Bob wants one of us to go with him to see the old man, and I think it should be you."

Lonny ambled in from the disco.

"What's wrong, guys?"

"Why don't you go back to your friends," Carl said harshly.

"What's wrong with him?" Lonny asked. He pointed a thumb at Carl.

Robert told him.

"Oh that poor man," Lonny said. "Can I come with you to see him?" he asked Carl.

"What are you going to do? Dance?"

The three of them looked at Carl and no one knew what to tell him or how to help him tell the old man, and they were sad for Carl and for the old man but they had not yet begun to think much about Joe.

"I'm going," Lonny said firmly, and Bob said, "We'd better go. It came over the radio awhile ago." Carl did not respond, but he walked toward the door and Lonny and Bob followed. Robert called in a bartender from the disco and he watched Carl and Lonny and Bob leave and he wiped the corners of his eyes with the sleeve of his caftan.

The three walked on the boardwalk toward the sea and then turned left toward the old man's house. Carl walked ahead. As he walked the boardwalk shook under his steps, but as they came closer to the house he slowed and lightened his

90

tread and Lonny left Bob's side and walked forward to Carl and he could see that Carl was holding back tears.

"You OK?" Lonny asked.

"Oh Christ, I can't do this." Carl's voice shook when he spoke.

Lonny put his hand on Carl's shoulder. "Yes, you can, and he'd rather hear it from you."

"Oh Christ," Carl said again, and then more softly, "I don't even know what happened," and he stopped and talked to Bob and tried to keep his voice steady and in its usual register, and he fought his urge to cry. Bob told him as much as he knew from the radio report: that the van had sped through a red light and hit Joe's car on the driver's side and that one of the two people in the van had also been killed and that it appeared that Joe had a broken neck.

Bob was embarrassed to tell it and he felt that he could easily be sick, and as Bob stood on the boardwalk in the declining hours of a late August afternoon and spoke Lonny put his arm around Carl's waist, and when Bob had finished and Carl had asked what questions he had and Bob had answered as well as he could, Lonny said to Carl, "You should tell him by yourself," and Carl answered, very quietly, "I know." Then they again walked, and the boardwalk did not shake under their feet.

The old man stirred when he heard the bell by the gate and thought, warmly, of Joe, and when the door in the kitchen opened he opened his eyes and called out, "You're back earlier than I expected."

"It's Carl," Carl called back, and he came into the front room and looked up at the loft. "I've got to talk to you."

The old man was surprised that Carl was in the house. He could not remember Carl ever coming in without being invited, and although he had just awakened he heard that Carl's voice sounded thin and shook a little.

"Hold on," he said. "I'll be right down."

He dressed, and while he dressed he wondered, and he thought that maybe there was a problem with Lonny and almost imperceptibly he had the quick-vanishing flash of an idea that it might involve Joe, and then he was dressed and he came down the steps.

Carl was standing by the old man's desk looking at the sea and at the sky, which was beginning to color. The old man walked over and stood beside him and looked too.

"Is anything wrong, Carl?" he asked, and Carl tried to speak but could not and he turned to the old man and the old man saw with surprise that Carl's face was red and that his eyes were filled with tears and that the corners of his mouth quivered, and the old man began to feel an uneasy apprehension. He swallowed heavily and with the tenderness of age held Carl by the shoulders and did not speak for a minute but just held, and then he spoke quietly and gently.

"What's happened?"

Carl faced him squarely and struggled to control his eyes and his mouth and his voice, and words did come.

"I'm sorry, so sorry," he said. Then tears started and his voice broke and still the old man did not know but he could feel a tension building in his stomach, and he swallowed heavily again.

"What happened?" The old man was more insistent this time.

Carl knew that he had to do it and he cried as much for the old man as for Joe, and finally he did do it.

"Oh God," he said, "it's Joe."

Now the old man felt as though he certainly would be sick and part of his mind started reeling off possibilities but had not reached the correct one before Carl told him. Carl had been trying to do it gently, but it did not come that way.

"He was in an accident. He's dead."

The old man felt a rush as adrenaline was released into his

system, increasing the rate of his heartbeat and the force of his heart's contractions and constricting his blood vessels, and his stomach felt as though he had accelerated over the crest of a hill and then dropped down the other side and his legs lost their strength and he began to tremble. He ran for the bathroom and was completely, exhaustively sick.

Carl sat in the kitchen, and when the sounds of the old man's sickness had subsided he got up and knocked on the bathroom door and asked the old man if he was all right, and the old man said yes and asked Carl to wait, and in a few minutes he came out. He looked gray, but he was composed and showed no tears. He walked slowly. He felt uncomfortably like he was falling and he held out his hand for the corner of the table. His hand and arm were not steady and when he sat his legs trembled. He faced Carl across the table and Carl knew that now it would be hard and he prepared himself.

"How do you know?" the old man asked.

"He carried a card that said to notify you if—"

The old man nodded. "I've got one that says to notify him."

"Well," Carl continued, "you don't have a telephone out here but the Sayville police knew you lived out here in the summer so they radioed over and Bob was in the office when they did it. He came to get me, and I wanted to tell you myself." Carl paused, and then he told the old man as many of the details as he knew, and always while Carl spoke the old man felt like he was falling.

When Carl was finished the old man asked about Bob, and Carl told him that Bob and Lonny were waiting out on the walk.

"Why don't you ask them in," the old man said.

"Are you sure?"

"I'm sure," the old man said, and Carl went outside and came back with them.

Bob was a young man, younger than Carl and younger than Joe, although not younger than Lonny, and he was embarrassed in the presence of someone who had been touched by death, and he was unsure of himself. His uniform and weapon did not give him the confidence they usually did.

"I'm sorry," he said.

"Yes," the old man replied, and he motioned for them to sit down, and they did. Lonny did not speak.

"Don't people usually drink coffee when someone dies," the old man said. He attempted a smile but it faded away, and he struggled with himself for control. He inhaled deeply.

"Would you like me to make some coffee?" Carl asked.

"Yes, please," the old man said, and Carl made coffee and the old man asked Bob questions and Bob told him the same things that Carl had.

While Bob talked the old man was gradually starting trying to remember and starting to remember, and he remembered many fragments but nothing for more than a second or two. The remembering was in no order and the old man was confused and felt like he was falling, and then a flash of memory became large and lucid and the reel of fragments stopped.

"Oh God. Has anyone told his family?" He looked at Bob and Bob shook his head.

"We can have someone take care of it," Bob said.

The old man tried to think. He called up a picture of Joe's mother and father and brother, but the picture was ten years old, and he remembered hard, mean words that had been said and he remembered hatred that had filled a room. He sighed and closed his eyes for a few seconds.

"No. I'll call them now," he said. "May I use your telephone?" he asked Carl.

"Sure. Do you want me to go with you?"

"No, I don't think so," the old man told him. "Why don't you wait here."

"OK. The door's open and you know where the phone is. Nobody's home so just go in."

The old man said thank you and he walked, a little

unsteadily, out the door and across the deck and up the board-walk toward Carl's house.

The old man walked slowly and although he knew that he was not he still felt faintly like he was falling. His thoughts came in bursts. Pretty marigolds. It's drier than usual this year. High-up gull. Rain tomorrow or the next day. Joe's had an accident. No more Alexander. Joe's father, what's he like now. Keep steady, keep steady. Person in van, how old. Funeral. Weather in Evanston in late summer. Carl's house. How much rent. Door needs rehanging. Lonny's shirt on chair. And now you've got to call, the old man told himself, yes I do and I must be calm. Joe's their son, brother too, but he's my son too, but that's different. I wonder what he looks like now. Broken probably, pale too. Not sleek and trim and easy like yesterday. Like a lump of clay maybe.

The old man was standing by the telephone now, and he picked it up. What's Chicago's area code, he thought. He called the operator for the area code and called information for the number. The information operator gave it to him.

"Wait," he said. "I don't have a pencil." He looked for a pencil and the operator said, "You'll have to call back, sir," and he still could not find a pencil or anything else to write with, and he could not remember the number either and the operator disconnected him.

"Bitch," he said. For a minute the anger soothed him, but then the anger faded and the feeling in his stomach came back strong. He was holding the receiver and it started to wail at him. He pushed the button on the telephone down and then called the local operator again.

"I need to reach Joseph Ross on Sheridan Road in Evanston, Illinois. It's an emergency."

The operator was a man.

"Do you have the number?" he asked.

"If I had the number why in hell would I be talking to

95

you," the old man snapped, and the anger returned briefly and was soothing.

"Is this an emergency?" the operator asked.

"Isn't the ability to hear a requirement for your job?" The old man's voice shook and the anger surged up.

"Just a minute please," the operator said. The old man could hear the operator call for the number and he heard the tones that meant that the number was being dialed and then he heard it ring. While it rang the operator told him the number for the next time he needed it and the anger, which had subsided, surged again.

A young man answered.

"Hello."

The old man concentrated hard now.

"Hello. Is this Scott?"

"Yes. Who is this?"

"This is Oswald Stevenson," the old man said. "May I please speak to your father."

"I'll ask him," Scott said.

The old man was not talked about in Scott's house and Scott, although he had only been ten at the time, could remember the old man's visit. The memory was not pleasant. He remembered men shouting and luggage being moved in and then out again, and he remembered that after Joe and the old man had left, his father had thrown out everything of Joe's that was left in the house. For the next few years whenever he had been asked about Joe his father had said, "I have no son named Joe," but now he simply said he didn't know.

"This is Joe Ross," the voice said. "I know you wouldn't call unless it was important, so what is it?"

"Joe's been in an accident."

The old man began to see a van speed slowly through a red light and push into the door of Joe's car, and he saw glass spray slowly, sparkling in the late afternoon sun, but he did not see the inside of the car.

"Can't you answer a simple question?" the voice said. "I asked you what kind of accident."

"A car accident," the old man said.

"Is he in the hospital?"

The old man saw the van slowly so slowly push the car away from it and he saw the metal crease and bend inward. He began to see inside the car then, too, and he knew that he could again be sick.

"Is he in the hospital?" the voice repeated.

"No," the old man said, so quietly.

"Is he there?"

"No."

"I can't hear you," the voice said. "Where is he?"

The old man had always been quick with words and now the first response that entered his consciousness was "heaven." He did not say it, and the thought of the response shamed him, but for an instant he forgot about the car and what was inside it. The thought and the shame were over quickly and he continued slowly:

"He didn't make it."

"My God! You mean he's dead?"

"Yes," the old man said. "I guess that's what it's called."

The voice was silent.

"Are you there?" the old man asked.

"Can I call you back in a few minutes?" Joe's father asked.

The old man said yes, and he read the number from the telephone and they said good-bye. The old man was thirsty and he went to the kitchen for water. While he waited for the water to run cold he began to think about people's life histories and their intersections and he waited for grief to come. He knew it would. He waited for it to wash over him like the sea and take him, but it was not yet time. His thoughts raced and flashed and part of him began to watch his thoughts race and flash, and his stomach felt as if he were falling. But there was

97

no grief, no lamentation. He drank the water slowly. He waited.

The telephone rang, and the old man was aware that a little time had passed but he could not remember it. He thought hard, trying to recapture his thoughts of a minute or two ago, and he again drifted away and the phone continued to ring.

Must answer it, Joe's father, he thought. His mind hovered outside and it told him yes you must answer it and you must think carefully and be calm, and the old man answered the telephone and part of him watched himself answer the telephone and listened to him talk and commented on his conversation.

"Hello."

"This is Joe Ross. I've got Joe's mother here and my son, my other son. Now can you tell me exactly what happened."

The old man told him what he knew. He told it flatly and the part that was hovering watching the part that was doing the telling approved. Joe's father asked for telephone numbers and the old man found a directory and gave him the numbers he asked for, and while he did this the part that was watching pressed the old man to think about the car, take a look. The part that was looking up the numbers and talking to Joe's father about schedules and arrangements firmly told the part that was watching that there would be time later, when he wasn't needed, to think, and to look inside the car, and the part that was watching said nothing but hovered a little farther away and watched and listened and remembered, and then he was through.

That door does need rehanging, the old man thought when he left Carl's house. He lifted the door by the knob so that it shut firmly, and the part of him that was hovering noticed that the exertion had caused his heart to beat a little faster, and the part that was thinking and remembering not

98

watching bubbled and tripped along and did not stop long on anything.

He walked back, acting normally the watching part told him. He said hello to two people he knew. Then the part that was thinking and remembering hit something and stopped and the part that was hovering watching came in and joined the part that was thinking and remembering and the old man remembered clearly a scene after his grandfather's death.

The old grandfather had been taken away, but then he was brought back in a reddish-brown–colored coffin and put in the parlor in front of a folding screen of pleated beige cloth. At both ends of the coffin were arrangements of flowers in high-standing containers whose lips spread to high fan-shaped backs behind the flowers. But what the old man remembered most vividly was the boy whom he once had been looking carefully at the figure in the coffin. The boy discovered that the figure had makeup on it, and the old man remembered the boy reaching out a finger to touch a cheek and jumping back when the cheek felt like wax.

And then the old man did not remember a strange boy in a distant room, but he remembered with immediacy a circle of large shadowy figures, adults, who watched and spoke in low tones. Then the part that had been hovering watching again moved out and watched and it pointed out to the old man the difference between remembering a boy who could have been someone else he was watching and remembering something as an immediate experience. The part that had been rushing, flowing, remembering, was released and rushed onward, darting here and there over times, and always another part was watching and hovering and the part that was watching and hovering pointed out to the old man that he felt a little like he was falling.

When the old man reached his gate it was open, and when he walked into the kitchen the part that was hovering and watching told him that Elizabeth was here and Bob was gone and Lonny was sitting on the counter.

Elizabeth got up and walked to the old man quickly and held his hand tightly.

"I guess you heard," the old man said, and he heard himself say it.

"Robert called me." Elizabeth looked into the old man's face. "How are you doing?"

"All right," he said. Tell her about falling, the hovering part told him. He sat down.

"I spoke to Joe's family."

"What's going to happen?" Elizabeth asked.

"Let's talk about that later," the old man said. "Not now."

"They're going to call me tomorrow at noon at your house," the old man told Carl. "Is that all right?"

"Of course. Just come over. I've got to work at lunch tomorrow, but I'll have Lonny stay around until noon just in case you don't get there on time or something." Carl looked over at Lonny, who nodded yes.

The old man turned to Elizabeth. "I gave them your number too."

"I'll tell Mildred," Elizabeth said.

The old man got a quick flash of an idea of an encounter between Joe's father and Mildred and the hovering watching part told him that it was funny and he smiled a little before the rushing part washed the idea away and rushed forward, confusedly.

"Where's Bob?" he asked.

"He had to go back," Carl told him. "He said to tell you that if there's anything he can do he'd be glad to."

The hovering part said how is he at miracles, but the old man just said, "If there is I'll let him know."

Elizabeth saw that the old man's face looked gray and that he acted weak and vacant, and she thought that she might give him some medicine she had brought with her to help him rest.

100

"I think he needs some quiet," she said to Carl and Lonny, and the old man did not disagree.

"Sure thing," Lonny said.

The old man was still sitting and Lonny jumped down from the counter and stood beside the old man's chair.

"Why don't I come back later and stay here tonight? I can sleep on the couch in the little room."

"It opens into a bed," the old man said. The hovering part told him you don't need him you're just feeling sorry for yourself, but the old man said, "If you want to come over that would be fine."

Lonny looked at Carl and Carl looked at Elizabeth and she nodded yes, and Lonny said that he would come and patted the old man's shoulder.

"See you later," he said.

The old man nodded.

Carl came to stand by the old man too. He looked down at him and Carl's eyes were liquid and full. The old man thought that Carl might say something that he did not want to hear and he stood up and held Carl's shoulder and shook his hand. Carl understood and he nodded, and he patted the old man's shoulder without speaking and turned his face away so that the old man could not see.

"Come on," Lonny said, and Carl nodded and did not speak and they left. Lonny gave the bell by the gate a ring on his way out.

"I'm worried about Carl," the old man told Elizabeth.

"And I'm worried about you," Elizabeth said. "I brought something I want you to take. It will relax you and keep your spirits up too."

"No," the old man said. "No drugs."

Elizabeth thought he should have it, but she decided to wait, so she said all right.

"Let's go out on the deck," the old man said. "It looks like it's going to be a good sunset."

101

The old man with the hovering part, and Elizabeth, went out onto the deck and sat in two of the canvas chairs. At first they did not speak, but then Elizabeth did.

"I'm really sorry. He didn't deserve it," she said.

The old man was quiet. He looked out to sea. We all die the hovering part said.

"We all die," he said.

There was something hard in his voice, and Elizabeth began to see that the old man was working and pushing within himself.

"It's all right to show some emotion," she said.

"Emotion is a private thing," the old man replied, and before and after he spoke and while he was speaking part of his mind ran like a stream and part of it hovered and watched.

Elizabeth felt sad for the old man, and for Joe, and she felt sad for Mildred and for herself too. She looked out to sea feeling sad and the old man looked out to sea trying not to feel sad and succeeding in not feeling anything. They watched the sea and the gold and orange that was expanding through the sky from the west, over their right shoulders, and the old man pointed to a low line of clouds and said that in a day or two it would rain. Elizabeth asked him about Joe's family and what was to be done.

"They're coming tomorrow. All of them," he said.

"Here?"

"In Sayville. They're renting a car at the airport and driving out. I gave them your number, or did I tell you that?"

"You told me. Are they taking Joe back to Evanston?"

"No," the old man said. The hovering part came back inside a little. "They're going to have something done here. Saturday, if possible."

"I'll come with you."

The hovering part flew back out and it watched the old man walking to the dock on Saturday and boarding the ferry and racing across the bay away from the island.

102

"No, I'm sorry. His family said no one but them and me."

"Are you going to be able to handle that?"

You're a tough guy, the old man told himself.

"Yes, I think so," he said.

"His family doesn't want any flowers," he added.

They sat and they did not talk. The old man thought about Joe, but not coherently, and he thought hard about their last conversation and the harder he thought the less he remembered and he tried to see a picture but the hovering part watched him trying to see and snatched it away. He tried now to feel sad because he could not remember, but the hovering part analyzed and told him that that was not genuine sadness and he tried harder and still felt nothing.

As he was trying to feel sad and thinking about trying to feel sad, another part was rushing on and it caught something and stopped and everything came together.

"You know," he said, "if you could make a graph with time on one axis and space on the other axis and have one colored line for Joe and a different colored line for the kid who died in the van the lines would wander all over the graph and then both end in one dot."

"I suppose so. What if they'd been in the same place at the same time before?"

The hovering part again hovered and something thought about Elizabeth's question and something else ran along on its own. The old man looked as though he might cry, but he held his forehead for a moment and the muscles in his face relaxed.

"Then the lines would have crossed, not ended." He thought a little. "Besides, the graph would have to have four axes, one for each of the three spatial coordinates and one for time."

Elizabeth looked carefully at the old man, and the hovering part of the old man said she's watching you like there's something wrong with you, and the old man looked away toward the east, away from the sky that was coloring with the sunset.

"Are you sure you're all right?" Elizabeth asked.

"I'm all right."

Tell her about feeling like falling the hovering part said.

"You know, a funny thing seems to be happening," the old man said. "I can almost feel part of me watching myself to see what I'm going to do and then commenting on it."

"I wouldn't worry about it," Elizabeth said gently. "I used to feel that way when I had a full practice. By the fourth or fifth patient I couldn't absorb much more but I knew I had to so I'd concentrate hard and part of my mind would watch me sitting there in the chair with my notebook and would make comments about the patients. Sometimes I think the patients would have run screaming from the room if they had known what I was thinking."

The old man forgot about the day a little.

"What did you think about when I was the patient talking to you?"

"I don't know. That was a long time ago, before—" Elizabeth fumbled for a word. "Well, it was a long time ago."

"You can say it. It was before Joe. I wish you, and everyone else, would just act naturally."

"No one knows how to act," Elizabeth said. "We all know you're hurt, and we're trying to be gentle."

"I know you are. But it still makes me uncomfortable."

The old man thought suddenly of time.

"It must be close to eight," he said.

Elizabeth looked at her watch. "Seven-thirty."

"I've known almost two hours," the old man said, looking at the sea. "I guess Bob isn't going to come back and tell me it was a mistake."

His voice faltered and Elizabeth thought that he might cry and she thought that would be good, but he did not. While he had been speaking part of him was remembering Joe's family

104

and thinking about their arrival, and he remembered what Joe had said about wanting to bring his brother to the island.

"Did you know that Joe's brother is ten years younger than Joe?" The old man paused. "Than Joe was, I guess."

"I knew he was younger, but not ten years younger."

"No, it's ten years. When Joe was in college his father told him that the reason his brother was ten years younger was that they had only intended to have Joe but that when Joe was ten his father knew that Joe was going to be the biggest disappointment of his life so he decided to try again. Joe's father told him, 'I wrote you off then, and I was right.'"

The old man looked out over the moving water and became aware that part was still hovering watching and another part was running on by itself, and he was tired and a little weak and in his stomach he still felt a little like he was falling.

Elizabeth thought about Joe's family. "I'm going with you on Saturday, or whenever you go to Sayville," she said.

"No, I'm sorry, but I've got to go alone," the old man said, and he sighed. Elizabeth shook her head, and she still intended to go.

"I'm getting tired," the old man told her.

"Have you had any dinner?"

The old man thought. "No, I guess I forgot."

"Let's go inside and I'll make you something." Elizabeth put her hand on the arm of the old man's chair.

The old man did not want to eat but he was beginning to feel very tired now, and he was too tired to argue. He stood up, heavily, and Elizabeth stood, and they went inside. Elizabeth went into the kitchen and the old man walked over to the table in the front room that held the bird of paradise flowers and looked at them for a few minutes and then went into the kitchen.

Dinner, the hovering part told him, was tasteless, although at the same time the old man remembered Gertrude Stein's proclamation that American food was moist and he

105

agreed that the food was moist; moist and tasteless the hovering part said. Elizabeth sat across the table from him. I wish she wouldn't watch me eat part of him thought, but the hovering part was watching him eat too and watching Elizabeth watching him eat, and the old man felt very tired.

He took a sip of mineral water and as he put down his glass it hit his plate and the part that was running in confusion and remembering heard the ring of the glass on the plate and matched it with another ring of a glass on a plate the night before. A small circle of clear memory opened and grew and the old man remembered Joe's face as it had looked in the candlelight at the restaurant and he heard Joe's voice as clearly as though Joe were in the room and had just stopped speaking and the sound of his voice was fading in the old man's ears. The old man remembered with a warmth and a sadness, but then he realized how clearly he was remembering and the circle closed and faded and his mind watched itself separate again.

"I'll put these pills over the sink when I leave, and I want you to take one before you go to bed," Elizabeth said. She showed him an envelope of pills. "I'll tell Lonny if he comes back before I go."

The old man did not say no, although he knew he would not take one. For the first time in hours he thought about writing and he told himself you must work tomorrow it's all you've got don't lose it, and while he was thinking about the next day part of him remembered a book he had once tried to write about unexpectedly dying young. He shuddered involuntarily.

"I feel like I've lived through this before," he said. "It wasn't until around the time I met Joe that I thought about there being two kinds of dying: the kind that is known about and prepared for, and the kind that is sudden and without warning."

"Tell me about it," Elizabeth said, and because the old man was tired and confused he found the ease that he had lost many years earlier of sitting with Elizabeth and just talking while she listened.

"Think about it," he said. "Almost everyone who writes about dying writes about the time when the character knows he's dying and those around him know he's dying, even if it's only known for a short time. Hemingway could make death seem gentle and kind, or glorious, but there was usually a scene where his character knows he's dying. I once tried to write a book about someone who was killed with no warning and about the trivial details of life shortly before and after."

Part of the old man's mind observed that he was being grim and he stopped.

"I just can't believe it yet, Elizabeth."

"It's hard to," she said softly.

"When I thought about death I imagined me leaving Joe and Joe living to be old like I am."

Elizabeth reached across the table and touched the old man's hand.

"I know it's hard, but you should be happy for the time you've had. Joe was a beautiful young man and the two of you together made everyone who knew you happy."

The old man thought that he would cry, but the hovering part told him no and instead he was hard.

"Now you sound like a sentimental old woman," he said roughly, and the hovering part was a little surprised at the way he said it.

Elizabeth had dealt with grief professionally many times and she understood the old man and knew that there was not much she could do to help now.

"You could use a little sentimentality too," she said. "You can't go through this being a stoic."

"Sadness is a very private thing," the old man answered slowly. He finished his dinner and still did not taste it. He was growing more tired and the hovering part was not hovering so much now. He did not feel fragmented, just tired and

107

confused and weak in his stomach. He drank warmed-up coffee while Elizabeth washed the dishes.

The bell by the gate rang loudly, and the old man looked through the window to see who it was.

"It's me," Lonny said when he walked in, and Elizabeth said hello, and the old man said hello and part of him watched himself say hello and observed that there was a space between the time he saw Lonny at the door and the time he said hello. The hovering part also told him that Elizabeth and Lonny had exchanged a look of some meaning, but it was a meaning that he could not read.

Elizabeth finished working at the sink and came back to the table and in herself she was feeling sad for the old man because she thought that he was now beginning to feel sad, and she knew that although he might struggle against feeling sad he would eventually lose the struggle and then it would be a heavy, hard time for him. She knew also that the old man would have to learn to live alone and to live only for himself and not for someone else too, and she knew that the old man had found joy in living for someone else in addition to himself, and she thought about how Joe had enjoyed living for the old man and had been protective and young and strong and loving and giving, and taking too, and proud for both of them. It was knowing all this that made her sad, and she could not completely keep the sadness from her voice.

The old man and Elizabeth talked for a while about the coming end of summer and about Elizabeth's practice and about the island and its changes and about Mildred, although not too much about Mildred because even in his own struggle with sadness the old man did not want to make Elizabeth feel sad. As they talked, Lonny sat on one chair with his feet on another. He was not feeling sad but was thinking about how lucky Joe and the old man had been. Lonny was accustomed to the sudden end of those times when his life was easy and pleasant, and therefore he did not think so much about the end of

108

Joe's and the old man's time together as about the time they had already had. He did feel a little sad for the old man, but it was not a sadness like Elizabeth's, which came from understanding. He was sad for the old man because he was old and would never find another Joe. The sadness that comes after physical rejection was the strongest kind of sadness that Lonny could imagine.

Gradually the old man began to find it an effort to talk to Elizabeth about the things that were not the thing he would not talk about then, and Elizabeth saw that it was beginning to be hard for the old man to sit and talk and she said that well she had better leave but that she would stop over the next day and that she would make sure that someone was at home in the morning in case Mr. Ross called.

"Take care of him for me," she told Lonny.

"Oh, I will," Lonny said, and he took his feet off the chair and walked over by the old man, who was still sitting.

Elizabeth started toward the door and the old man started to stand.

"Oh don't get up. Lonny can walk me to the gate," Elizabeth said.

"Sure," Lonny said, and the old man said, "OK, I'll see you tomorrow." He sounded old and tired and Elizabeth came back to where he was sitting and looked down at him and then bent down and kissed his cheek.

"I'm so sorry," she said. Her voice was not strong.

"I know. Thank you." The old man sighed heavily. "Now get going. Mildred must be waiting for you."

Elizabeth said good-bye and motioned to Lonny, and the two of them walked out the door and across the deck. The old man watched through the window.

"Try to get him to take one of the pills I left," Elizabeth told Lonny. "They're on the windowsill over the sink."

"I'll try," Lonny said, but he did not think that it was as important as Elizabeth did.

"And call me if there is anything wrong. I don't care if it's in the middle of the night."

"I will," Lonny said. He pulled the gate open for Elizabeth. The evening had grown cooler and Lonny shivered a little in his T-shirt.

"I've got to get inside," he said. "I'll talk to you tomorrow."

Elizabeth walked through the gateway. "Take care of him," she said, and she walked down the boardwalk toward the center of the Grove.

Lonny closed the gate and went back into the house. The old man was sitting as he had been when Elizabeth had left, in a straight-backed chair turned a little away from the table. He was no longer looking through the window; his eyes were closed.

"You OK?" Lonny asked.

The old man opened his eyes and spoke slowly. "That's not an easy question to answer."

"Listen, if I were you I'd have a drink and go to bed," Lonny said. "Nothing looks right when you're tired, and you look beat."

The old man smiled thinly. "Nothing's going to change in the morning."

"No, but it will look different. Now where's the booze?" Lonny asked, although he already knew. "I'll fix you a drink."

Part of the old man said why are you letting this kid decide things for you, you don't need him or a drink and stop feeling sorry for yourself, and part of him was remembering Joe and his brashness when he had been younger, and part analyzed and understood that Joe's brashness had been calculated, intelligent manipulation and that Lonny's was not and he realized that Lonny's brashness was a genuine response to the old man's situation.

"It's in the cupboard." The old man motioned. "How about some scotch and some ice. Make one for yourself too."

Lonny opened the cupboard and looked at the bottles. "Hey, you've got some good stuff here. I don't mind if I do." He took down a bottle of twenty-one-year-old scotch and put it on the counter.

"Glasses are in there." The old man pointed.

Lonny got down two glasses, filled them with ice, and brought the glasses and the bottle to the table.

"Say when," he said, pouring.

"When, when!" the old man said as Lonny filled his glass. Lonny pushed the glass toward the old man and poured himself a generous portion too.

"Boy, that's smooth," Lonny said after he took a sip.

The old man nodded. "Joe never liked scotch much," he said.

"Me, I'll drink anything."

The old man did not respond, but was tripping along remembering and thinking and watching Lonny all at the same time. Then he heard what Lonny had said.

"Not Joe. He wasn't much for alcohol."

"Did he do drugs?"

The old man thought for a few seconds. "Not very much. He smoked pot once in a while, but that was about it." The old man smiled a little at a memory. "He got me to try it once too, but I didn't feel anything."

"You didn't do enough," Lonny said. He took a drink from his glass and wiped his mouth with the back of his hand.

"Do you smoke pot much?" the old man asked, more out of politeness than interest, and while he asked it part of him commented what do you care what the kid does, he could drink hemlock for all you care. The old man shifted in his chair and looked at Lonny.

"Not too much," Lonny answered. "Usually only to top off an evening. You know, after a couple of 'ludes and a couple of martinis and some poppers you start to drag a little, so you take a hit or two."

The old man shook his head. "That doesn't sound like a good time to me."

"Each to his own." Lonny raised his glass. "Say," he said, "are you going to use those pills Elizabeth left?"

"No, this scotch is plenty and I don't like to take drugs anyway."

"Can I have them?"

The old man tried to think about that, but he was too tired to think clearly and still in his stomach he felt like he was falling.

"I guess so," he said. "But don't tell Elizabeth I gave them to you."

"Hey, thanks. I won't tell." Lonny got the envelope of pills and brought it back to the table.

"I wonder what they are," he said, examining the capsules. "They're mean-looking little gray things."

"I could ask Elizabeth tomorrow," the old man offered.

"No, that's all right. I'll use them sometime when I'm in the mood for a surprise."

The old man rubbed his eyes and Lonny saw that he looked old, very old, and tired.

"Com'on, it's past your bedtime," Lonny said. He took the old man by the arm and the old man did not protest or resist and they walked into the big room. The old man went into the little room under the loft and turned on the light.

"That couch opens out into a bed," he told Lonny. He showed him where sheets and towels were.

The old man realized then that Lonny had brought nothing with him. "Do you need to get anything at Carl's?" he asked.

"Nope. This is all I need." Lonny pulled a toothbrush out of the pocket of his jeans and held it up.

"Let's go say good night to the sea," he said, and he took the old man's arm and they walked out on the deck. The sky was mostly filled with clouds and only a few stars were visible. The wind off the ocean was moist and cool and salt-smelling.

"It will rain in the next day or two," the old man said. He shivered, and he thought that grief was finally coming to take him as he had been expecting, but the hovering part hovered and watched and kept the grief at bay.

"I'm sorry about Joe," Lonny said, and then it was the right thing to say. The old man nodded and he found in Lonny a comfort.

Lonny pointed up at a star and said quietly, half to himself, "Star light star bright I wish I may I wish I might have the wish I wish tonight."

The old man heard and part of him wondered what Lonny would wish for and then he did his own wishing and the end of his strength drained out of him and there was no longer any hovering or running or tripping along, but only a closing, coming darkness.

"I've got to go to bed," he said, and Lonny held his arm as they walked inside and he watched while the old man climbed the steps to the loft.

"Do you want to brush your teeth?" Lonny said.

"Not tonight," the old man said quietly and heavily.

Lonny waited for a minute and when he heard the old man get into bed he went into the bathroom and brushed his own teeth carefully, and when he was finished brushing he looked at his teeth in the mirror. Then he went into the kitchen, refilled his glass with scotch, and went out onto the deck and listened to the sea.

The old man lay still in bed and for the first time he began to feel alone, and he began to feel very sad. His sadness was not a grieving at his own loss but rather a heavy sadness for what had happened to Joe. Now the old man allowed his imagination to run freely and he thought about the accident again and again, only now he did not see it as a slow event accompanied by a soundless slow shower of glass but he saw

113

and heard it quickly and loudly; he heard the crash of machines and the screams and he felt more strongly the sinking feeling in his stomach. As he lay there he could hear the sea and gradually it lulled him toward sleep. At first the sound of the waves made him hear the crash of the cars again and again, but as he approached the border of sleep the crash of steel and glass grew softer until the sound of the sea overcame it.

While the old man slept he rolled and jerked spasmodically and he dreamed of the sea. He sat on the beach and out in the water he could see Joe swimming back and forth with slow steady strong practiced strokes. He doesn't know, the old man thought in his dream, I've got to tell him. At first he tried calling, but always he saw the arms come out of the water and then enter it again, smoothly and steadily, and Joe did not hear. I've got to tell him the old man thought, I've got to tell him, and he walked out into the water. He took no precautions in the face of the breaking waves and the surf pushed him down and fell over him and he felt himself falling. He fell through the dark green water slowly, tumbling unevenly and unable to stop his fall. But gradually the fall slowed and stopped and up through the water he could see light and he pulled hard for the light and he felt as though his lungs might burst. When he broke the surface he shook his head and the water fell from his long white hair slowly, like a gentle shower of glass. He saw Joe still swimming steadily but farther away and again he tried to call, and again a wave pushed him down and he fell slowly toward the deep and then slowly swam up, and when he broke the surface the water streamed slowly from his hair like a shower of glass and he was no closer to Joe. In his dream he fell through the water and fought back to the surface and fell and fought back, and he grew more and more tired and each time he fell farther and the swim to the surface grew longer, and each time he broke the surface it was a little darker above the water and Joe was swimming farther and farther away. Finally when he came up Joe was

114

gone and it was almost totally dark and the old man cried out in his dream because he had been unable to tell Joe that he was dead, and he felt a bottomless feeling of loss. The cry woke the old man a little and it stopped the falling through the water, but he continued to sleep a ragged, troubled sleep.

The old man awoke early in the morning. Already the hovering part of him was at work and when he was only semiconscious it reminded him of the thing he did not want to know, and he did not forget and reach out for Joe. He got up feeling sad and tired; his stomach did not feel right and his head felt tight. He climbed down from the loft and went into the kitchen and then, after he had already remembered, he forgot, and he was surprised that there was no water or coffee in the coffee maker, and the hovering part reminded him again and told him that he needed to be strong but he did not feel very strong.

He measured the coffee and the water and started the coffee maker going and then went to shower. He ran the water warm when he stepped in and gradually increased the amount of hot water until the water was quite hot and the room filled with steam. The heat was relaxing and for a few minutes he did not feel bad and he started to hum a little. However, part of him caught himself starting to sing and asked how he could sing when Joe was lying in a refrigerator somewhere over on Long Island, and the old man began to feel sad again and he did not sing.

When he came out of the bathroom he felt weary and again his head hurt. The coffee maker had done its job and the kitchen smelled brownly, pleasantly, of coffee and the old man again forgot what he had remembered and he went to the cupboard and took out two mugs and put them on the counter. Then, when he looked at the mugs he thought he might cry and almost did, but the hovering part held him back and told

115

him to be strong and that an old man would look foolish crying, and he did not cry. He turned away.

The bottle of scotch was still on the table from the night before, and the old man put it away and then went back to the counter. He looked at the mugs carefully. They were decorated with paintings of large oriental-looking cats staring into fishbowls and had been a gift to Joe from a friend who knew Joe didn't care much for cats, at least not the small domestic variety. The old man felt sad and the hovering part told him that it was just the beginning of the day and that the day would be hard. Buck up, he told himself. He shivered a little and drew his robe more tightly around him. Then he poured a mug of coffee and went to dress.

In the front room he noticed that the bird of paradise flowers had opened beautifully and were vividly blue and orange. You've got a bunch of flowers not Joe, the hovering part told him, and in his sadness the beauty of the flowers was enhanced and crushing. He stood and looked at the flowers and started to remember again. He remembered a white, tropical beach where kumquats fell from the trees lining the beach and rotted sweetly in the sun, and he remembered a young, tanned man with red-brown hair and an old tanned man with white hair who lay on the beach together and then later snorkeled in the water, and as the old man remembered Joe swimming lazily beside him, pointing out exotic fish and coral, he remembered his dream and his sadness grew and his memories seemed dreamlike and unreal.

The old man caught himself standing by the table that held the flowers and he realized he had been standing there for a few minutes. Now don't fall apart he told himself, and he climbed to the loft.

When he came back down the door of the room Lonny had slept in was open and the old man looked in. Lonny was sitting on the bed, wearing jeans but barefoot and shirtless. He was rubbing his eyes.

116

Be polite, the old man told himself, and he said "Good morning."

"Morning," Lonny said. He looked at the old man. "You don't look so good."

The old man rubbed the corners of his eyes. "How do I look bad?"

"Oh, you just look tired. Why don't you go back to bed for a while?"

"I couldn't sleep if I did. But anyway, I want to work."

Lonny stood up and rolled the shirt and underwear that he had been wearing the night before into a bundle.

"Why don't you take it easy for a few days," he said.

You've got to write now or you never will, the old man told himself. "No, I've got to write, at least a little," he said. He found the thought of writing comforting because it meant following part of his daily routine, and at the same time he wondered if he would be able to write, and the two thoughts made him anxious to sit at his desk and try it.

"Help yourself to anything you want," he said. "I'm going to try to work now."

"That's OK. I've got to go back to Carl's and shower and get some clean clothes and things. I'll eat there."

The old man was still standing in the doorway and Lonny stepped into his moccasins, picked up his clothes, and came and stood in front of him. Lonny was young and thin and shirtless and his closeness made the old man suddenly ache for Joe. He wanted to touch Lonny for comfort, to feel his warm skin and think of Joe, but instead he turned away and walked to his desk and sat down. Lonny watched from the doorway and then walked over and stood by the old man.

"Listen," he said. "I'm a friend, right?" He stopped and looked at the old man. The old man nodded and he felt tears beginning to rise. "So if you need anything, just tell me, OK?"

The old man turned toward the sea. Christ, he thought,

117

I'm finally going to lose it and it's going to be in front of the kid, and part of him said tell him to go away, and without turning away from the sea the old man said thickly, "I've got to work."

"Sure thing," Lonny said. "I'll come back later." He patted the old man's shoulder and then rested his hand there, and the old man patted the hand on his shoulder but did not turn around.

"Bye," Lonny said. He gave the old man's shoulder a final pat and went out toward the kitchen and then out the door facing away from the sea. He gave the bell by the gate a good ring on his way out, and when the old man heard it he smiled a little through his sadness.

He watched the sea for a long time. Lonny's youth and vitality made the old man again think of Joe, and he moved his hand in the air in a caress, and he remembered Joe's smooth skin and his long hair and the way he was formed and the way he looked and walked and swam, the way he felt to touch, but he could not quite remember the way he talked. As he remembered, it all seemed more and more incomprehensible and unbelievable and part of him for the first time began to think about what the remainder of his life would be like without Joe, and then too for the first time he began to think about not living also, and as he thought this his eyes filled. Now stop that he told himself, and he wiped his eyes with the back of his hand and pulled his chair into his desk. He did not cry.

Joe's dead and you're not and that's that, he told himself. And you must write now because if you do not it will be harder tomorrow and then even harder each day after that. You can't help Joe the old man told himself, and he realized that he was being hard and he sat stiffly at his desk and tried to relax and he invited the waves of emotion to come and wash over him and take him away but they did not come, and he felt unfulfilled.

Finally he opened the top drawer of his desk and took out

118

his pen and his glasses and the folder of yellow pages. As he always did, he first read what he had written the day before. It's not that bad, he thought, and he took up his pen and began to write. Although he was writing a book that was mostly about a young man he did not for a while think of Joe. He had trained himself through the years he had been writing to always start work as soon as he took out the paper, and so for a while he wrote quickly and instinctively, and it was good. Then, as he often did, he took off his glasses and looked out to sea and while he watched the moving surface he again thought of Joe. He began then to truly understand that he would now always be alone and that he could not bring Joe back, and in his stomach he again began to feel like he was falling.

Earlier that morning he had thought about ending his own life, but then it had been a quickly discarded idea thrown up to the surface by the turmoil in his mind. Now he began to think seriously of it and he thought about how he might do it. Pills and booze? I could probably get enough he thought from Lonny and Elizabeth, but it's too uncertain, and part of him told himself that it was a coward's way. Gun? No, then there's a mess. He looked out to sea and slowly the idea grew until it had a life of its own and began to become a certainty. I can swim straight out until I can't swim anymore he thought. No mess, probably no body, and I love the sea. He did not think about being afraid.

He thought more about dying and, although the hovering part told him he was enjoying the thought a little, he thought about how everyone would then know and say how much he had cared for Joe. He became sad at the thought of his own death, but it was an indulgent kind of sadness that included imagining how sad others would be, and although he was aware of it this new kind of sadness overcame his sadness for Joe. His eyes filled a little, but even then the hovering part did not allow him to cry, so instead of washing away this new sadness for himself and with it some of the sadness for Joe he

119

nurtured them both. He planned how they would end together, and the planning was comforting.

It was an overcast day and the sea looked gray. The old man allowed his eyes to blur and lost himself in the sea's movement and in the sound of the surf. He thought about his decision and the part of him that he could feel watching himself did not disagree. He thought about ancient customs of slaughtering people to provide companionship in another world for someone who had died, and then he remembered reading about the excavations at Ur, which had been recent when he had been in college and had excited scholars and students alike.

At Ur ranks of attendants and guards had been killed and buried with the queen. Their bodies were found in orderly arrays and were dressed in finery. A musician was found with her hands on her lyre, and teams of oxen had been led down into the burial pits dragging carts and then killed with their grooms at their heads. Nowhere was there a sign of a struggle, just a calm, orderly death. The old man thought about the burial ceremonies at Ur and he wondered if the people who had accepted their murder in the tomb so calmly had been drugged, and he thought about joining Joe and he thought that oblivion would be welcome.

The old man wrote no more. He put his pen and papers and glasses into the desk, and he watched the sea, and then he got up and brought the vase of flowers to his desk and while he admired them part of him began to trip along and remember, and a heavy sadness for Joe returned. He began to feel a little helpless because he could not do anything for Joe and because of his decision about the sea. However, the hovering part held him firm and he thought about when he would join the sea and it was again some comfort to him.

The bell by the gate drew him away from his thoughts and away from the sea, and he heard the door in the kitchen open and he heard Lonny say as he walked in:

"It's me."

"Hello," the old man said. He turned toward Lonny as Lonny walked into the room and over to the desk.

"Joe's father just called for you," Lonny said. "I told him I'd get you. You're supposed to call him back."

The old man rubbed his eyes. "It can't be noon."

"Yup. Almost ten after."

The old man felt the puzzled uncomfortable feeling that comes from losing a block of time. He tried to remember how the time had passed, but he could not.

"You all right?" Lonny asked.

"I guess so. I thought it was around ten."

The old man got up slowly. He stroked one of the flowers as he did.

"Do you have the number?" he asked.

"I wrote it down back at the house."

"Let's go then," the old man said, and they walked out the door and across the deck to the gate and turned right toward Carl's house. Lonny rang the bell as they left.

When they reached Carl's house Lonny found the paper on which he had written the number and gave it to the old man, who held the paper in one hand and the receiver against his shoulder and dialed with his free hand. Lonny stood watching and the old man stopped and looked hard at him.

"Sorry," Lonny said, and he went into another room and then outside. The old man finished dialing the number.

First he got a switchboard operator and then there was a click and there was a ringing and then Joe's father answered.

"Joe Ross," he said. His voice was deep and hoarse, and a little slurred from tiredness.

"Hello, this is Oswald Stevenson," the old man said. "I'm sorry I missed your call. I was working."

The old man realized as he said "working" that it might not seem like an appropriate thing to be doing, and Mr. Ross

121

thought cold-blooded bastard how could he be working, and there was a short uncomfortable silence.

"Did you have any problems getting here?" the old man asked.

"No. We caught a six-o-five flight and were out here by ten. We're at that place you recommended on the bay, by the mouth of the channel."

"I know," the old man said.

"Oh, I guess you'd have to."

They were again silent and the old man did not want to push Joe's father so he waited.

"Well," Mr. Ross said, "I settled everything on the telephone last night." He told the old man that it would be on Saturday, the funeral, and exactly when and where it would be, and that he had arranged for an Episcopal priest, and he told the old man that after there would be no body, only ashes.

"Joe would have liked that," the old man said. It was the first time during their conversation that either the old man or Mr. Ross had referred to Joe by name. The old man could not keep a tenderness and a sadness from his voice and Mr. Ross heard it and did not like it and the old man knew he had heard it and had not liked it.

"Listen," Mr. Ross said. "This is going to be private. Just my son, my wife, and you. No one else."

The old man knew what he meant and he knew that it would be hard for Mr. Ross to see him and harder for him to see a group of Joe's friends.

"I know," he said. "I've already told people that."

There was another silence and the old man thought about the next day.

"Would you like to come over here after?" he asked, "to see where he lived? We could catch the ferry around three and you could go back when you wanted to."

"We couldn't stay all night," Mr. Ross said quickly. "We fly back early on Sunday."

"That's all right," the old man told him.

"Wait a minute."

The old man heard the muffled sounds of a discussion and then Mr. Ross was back on the telephone.

"Yes, we would like to come."

The old man suddenly found the conversation, short as it had been, very tiring. "All right, we'll talk tomorrow," he said.

"Do you want me to pick you up at the ferry?" Mr. Ross asked.

"Why don't I meet you at your motel. The ferry is just down the street."

"That's fine too," Mr. Ross said.

"About noon?"

"Fine."

"I'll be there," the old man said, and then they both said good-bye, and after they hung up they each stayed by the telephone and tried to visualize the man they had been speaking to.

Tomorrow's going to be a day the old man thought and he thought about joining the sea and he thought that Saturday night would be the time. He went to look for Lonny.

Although it was an overcast day Lonny was lying on the beach in front of the house. The old man came down to the sand and stopped to take off his shoes. He walked barefoot toward Lonny, and Lonny looked up as he approached.

"All set?" Lonny said.

"I guess you could say that. Thanks again for coming to get me."

"No sweat," Lonny said. "Want to sit down?" he asked. He squirmed sideways until there was an empty spot on his towel.

"Not now. I have to get back."

"Want me to come?" Lonny asked.

"No. That's all right," the old man said. "You can stop over later if you want," he added.

"OK," Lonny said, and the old man said "See you later then," and he walked up the beach toward the dunes and when he reached the walk, which there ended in a ramp down to the sand, he brushed off his feet with his hand and put his shoes back on.

The old man realized that his house would be empty and he did not want to be in an empty house then, so he decided to walk to the post office and through the center of the town where there would be people and activity. He started walking and instead of taking the most direct route he walked on a route that would take him past Robert's house because he thought that he might see Robert outside. He was beginning to feel more alone now.

As he walked, again part of him hovered and watched himself and noticed the weak boards in the boardwalk and heard the gulls and told him he did not need to see Robert, and part of him remembered the now long-ago confrontation with Joe's father, and he remembered that although he had told himself he would not argue he had called the man a perfect example of an American primitive when the man had said that his son was a dumb faggot. Yes the old man thought, tomorrow would be a day a long day and part of him thought that it would be his last day, and again the two kinds of sadness, for himself and for Joe, joined and provided a foundation for the remembering and the watching.

Robert's house lay about halfway between the sea and the bay. A narrow boardwalk led to the house from the public walk, and it widened into a deck that surrounded the house. The deck was surrounded by pines and thickets of salt-spray roses and as the old man passed he saw Robert outside cutting some of the roses and he thought that in his caftan Robert

124

looked like Gertrude Stein. The old man walked slowly and Robert saw him and put down his pruning shears and his roses and took off his gloves and hurried out toward the old man. His caftan fluttered around and behind him, but he was without beads.

"I've been thinking about you," he said as he came up to the old man.

The old man smiled a little and was glad that Robert had been outside and had seen him.

"How are you?" he asked.

"Never mind me. How are you?"

Part of the old man said tell him about the sea, but he did not. "I'm OK," he said. "A little tired, I guess."

"Have you had lunch?" Robert asked.

"I never eat lunch in the summer," the old man said. "You know that."

"Well, this time you should. You need to keep strong. Come on, I'll fix you something."

"No. Thank you anyway, though."

"Well at least sit down then," Robert said, and the old man agreed and they walked to the side of the house and sat in two white wrought-iron chairs.

The old man did not talk at first, but sat and remembered and watched himself and was comforted to be near an old familiar friend. Then he began to speak a little of Joe.

"God, I miss him already," the old man said. His hand was on the arm of his chair and Robert did not reply but put his hand on top of the old man's. The old man did not look at Robert but continued to talk.

"There are so many things I wish I could do over. Just yesterday I was arguing with him about Alexander the Great, who was one of his heroes. I wish I could tell him that I don't give a damn about Alexander or anything else. God, Joe didn't even live as long as Alexander did."

The old man's voice started to break. Take it easy he told

125

himself, and "Take it easy," Robert said, and the old man settled into his chair and was quiet.

"Carl told me that everything was going to be private," Robert said after a while.

"It is. Joe's parents and brother are over in Sayville now. I just spoke with his father."

"Didn't you have some trouble with him once?"

"Yes," the old man said sadly, and part of him felt like talking and part of him told himself to stop looking for sympathy.

The old man remembered the arguments and the threats and the names, and he remembered that although he had been trapped into it he had strongly defended Joe and himself and that at first when they had left Joe's house it had been rough between him and Joe but gradually he had become glad and then proud that Joe had done it. He did not share this with Robert.

"His father tried to get me fired," he said.

"What'd you do?"

"Not too much. I told the university that Joe and I were both adults and that I had been a successful writer before I taught at Yale and would be if I left, and I offered to leave."

"No one would want to lose you," Robert said.

"I'm not sure you speak for Joe's father. You know, when I spoke to him yesterday it was the first time since I left his house."

"God, how was it?"

"Not too bad," the old man said. "They're coming over here tomorrow afternoon," he added.

"Do you want moral support?"

At first the old man thought no, and as he thought it he realized that he would be embarrassed to have Joe's father meet some of his friends, and when he thought this he was ashamed and then he thought why not.

"Certainly, come over. We should be back on the three

o'clock ferry." Even in his sadness the old man began to enjoy the thought of Joe's father meeting a man in a caftan.

"I'll ask Lonny and Carl, and Mildred and Elizabeth too," he said.

"Don't worry, I'll dress civilly," Robert told him.

"Don't do that." The old man thought for a few seconds. "Could you have some food brought over from the restaurant?"

"I'm sure. What do you want?"

"You pick," the old man said. "Food for eight or ten. You can send the stuff over while I'm, I'm—" The old man stumbled on the thought. "While I'm over in Sayville. You can put it on our—" He swallowed. "—our bill. The key is over the door, you know."

"I'll take care of it," Robert said.

Part of the old man wanted to stay and cling to Robert's voice and company, but part of him was uncomfortable that he had been away from the house so long and wanted to move around and get back home where he would be closer to Joe.

"I'm going to go," he said as he stood up. "Thanks for seeing about the food."

"Maybe I'll stop in later," Robert said, and the old man said that would be fine and he walked out toward the main walk and waved good-bye.

He's not himself, Robert thought, and as he was thinking this, part of the old man was thinking about the next day and part of him was thinking about the pile of roses back on the table outside Robert's house. The old man turned back.

"What are you going to do with all those roses?" he asked.

"I'm going to make rose water."

"What do you do with rose water?"

"I'm making a rose cake."

"Oh," the old man said, and he said good-bye again and turned and walked away while Robert watched.

127

He walked slowly toward the bay and then turned toward the center of town. He thought about Joe and about not-being. He remembered an operation he had once had when he had been under anesthesia for more than an hour but the point at which he had come out had been immediately joined to the point at which he had gone under. He thought that death must be like that missing time when he was under anesthesia and he thought about it until he could not anymore, and thinking about the missing time began to bring back the feeling in his stomach that he was falling. He thought about joining the sea and about the moment when he would drift out of consciousness and he thought that, unlike losing consciousness with anesthesia, then there would be nothing to connect that final moment of consciousness to.

While he was walking and thinking he saw several people whom he knew and who knew him and part of him noticed that, while some of them did say hello and one did say he was sorry, others seemed embarrassed and anxious to avoid him. I've felt the same way he thought. Why? Why be embarrassed in the presence of someone who is suffering through a death? Suffering, a good word. I guess that's what I'm doing. Would I feel differently if there had been some transition time between Joe living and Joe not? A disease, cancer maybe. Better for Joe this way; no suffering for him, just for me. I guess I'm doing it for him; now he'll never have to grieve for me. And always, while the old man walked, part of him noticed the boardwalk and the houses and the people and the gray sky and smelled the sea in the air.

The old man stopped at the post office and part of him was disappointed that there was no mail and part of him said why do you care, and he left the post office and walked on. He reached the center of town shortly after the ferry landed, and the walk was filled with young men and a few old men and a few women. Everyone talked loudly and laughed and carried bags and boxes and someone led a dog and they were all eager

128

to join the life of Cherry Grove. The flow of people made the old man want to get away and he quickly walked through the town and turned down the walk toward his house, and as he walked he was again aware that people noticed him and also that they spoke about him and he knew they knew about Joe.

When he reached his house he found the gate open. Elizabeth and Mildred were sitting on the bench by the door that led into the kitchen, and there was a picnic basket on the deck beside the bench.

"We brought you some things," Elizabeth said and as she was speaking Mildred got up and walked to the old man. She held both of his hands tightly and looked into his face.

"I know everybody says this, but I'm really sorry for you. I liked Joe. He was my favorite young man."

The old man said thank you. I'm sure Joe didn't know that, he thought.

Elizabeth joined them and the old man took one of his hands away from Mildred and gave Elizabeth's hand a squeeze, and his eyes filled but he controlled it.

"Why didn't you go inside?" he asked. His voice was husky.

"It's locked," Mildred said.

"I don't remember doing that." The old man walked to the door and turned the handle. "I guess it is," he said. He reached over the door and took down a key and opened it.

"Come in," he said, and they went inside.

Mildred set the basket on the table.

"Want a drink?" the old man asked her.

She looked at her watch. "It's almost two." She sounded undecided.

"No," she said, "later," and she pulled out a chair from the table and sat with her arms crossed.

"We thought you might not feel like shopping, so we did it," Elizabeth said. She started taking things from the basket and putting them on the table. There was pâté wrapped in

129

plastic wrap and a cooked chicken in a bag and cheese and Perrier water and some bread.

"Would you like me to put it away?" she asked.

The old man was hungry but could not think about eating.

"Please," he said, and he sat across the table from Mildred, who looked seriously at him.

"Are you OK, sweetie?" she asked.

The old man inhaled deeply and exhaled slowly.

"Why is everyone asking me if I'm OK? I'm fine. I wasn't in an accident; I've been sitting here in comfort. Of course I'm OK."

Part of the old man observed that he had spoken sharply.

"Now take it easy," Mildred said. "You may think you're OK, but you look ready to drop. Did you sleep last night?"

"Did you take the pills I left?" Elizabeth asked. She was putting things in the refrigerator and her back was toward the old man.

"I slept all right," the old man said. As he said it part of him remembered his dream about falling through the water and crying out when Joe had disappeared, and as he remembered it an inextinguishable sense of loss welled up in him as it had during his dream. The sadness for Joe returned.

"Have you had lunch?" Elizabeth asked.

"I don't eat lunch in the summer." The old man tried to remember if he had eaten breakfast.

"Today, you do," Mildred said, and she started to stand up.

"I'll make something," Elizabeth said, and Mildred settled back down.

"What would you like?" Elizabeth asked.

"I'm not really hungry," the old man said, although he was.

"Well, then I'll just fix something and you can eat what you want to."

The old man was too tired to argue, and while Elizabeth took things back out of the refrigerator and busied herself at the counter he leaned back in his chair and closed his eyes.

The bell by the gate rang, and then Lonny opened the kitchen door without knocking and walked in.

"Hi," Lonny said.

"Scram," Mildred said.

Lonny's smile faded and he stopped and looked at the old man.

"Come in, come in," the old man said.

"Don't you knock?" Mildred demanded. She looked hard at Lonny, but he did not answer. He pulled out a chair and sat by the old man. Elizabeth brought over a plate of assorted foods and put it in front of the old man along with a glass of juice and a fork.

"Looks like a cocktail party," Lonny said.

"Have some." The old man motioned, and he pushed the plate between them.

"Can I have a fork?" Lonny asked. Elizabeth brought him one and then sat down across the table from them, next to Mildred. Lonny worked on the old man's lunch and Mildred stared steadily. The old man took a few bites and watched Mildred and Lonny and was amused, and for a while the sadness withdrew to the background although it did not leave.

"Did you talk to Joe's father?" Elizabeth asked. "He didn't call us."

"Yes. Everything is settled. It's tomorrow at twelve-thirty. There's no burial; he's going to be cremated." The old man spoke expressionlessly and almost coldly, and he went on:

"His family is coming over here after. Around three-thirty. I'd like you to come over too, if you can."

"We'll come," Elizabeth said. "Can we do anything while you're off the island?"

"Isn't his father a real prick?" Mildred interrupted.

131

The old man relaxed a little and smiled. "He was once. I don't know about now.

"That's all right," he said to Elizabeth. "Robert is sending some food over from the restaurant."

"He's another one," Mildred said.

The old man smiled again and part of him saw himself smile and he stopped.

"Now be kind," Elizabeth said.

They heard the bell and through the windows they watched Carl come across the deck. He was carrying a large pan covered with foil. The old man got up and met him at the door.

"Come in."

Carl came in.

"Robert sent you this. It's roast beef." He put the pan on the counter. He seemed embarrassed. "Hello everybody," he said.

"Hi," Lonny answered. He had finished most of the old man's lunch.

"Hey, you had lunch at the restaurant," Carl said.

"I'm just a growing boy."

Lonny smiled and Mildred looked as though she was priming herself for an outburst, but the old man spoke first.

"I wonder why everyone brings food when someone dies." He thought a little. "I can never remember a time of death when there wasn't food. When my grandfather died people brought something called funeral pie. It had raisins in it." The old man started to think about Joe again and the sadness came back into the foreground.

There was a silence.

"Well, I've got to work again at dinner," Carl said. "So I guess I'll go home and rest for a while." He was uncomfortable in the old man's presence. "You coming?" he asked Lonny.

"Not now. I'll come later, or I'll stop in at the restaurant."

Carl looked at the old man. "Would you like to be left alone for a while?"

Part of the old man said yes he would, he could then remember the past and think about the sea without interruption, but part of him knew that he did not want to be alone and that it was pleasant to have Lonny there because Lonny wasn't so damned reverent for his sadness.

"That's all right," he said. "Maybe Lonny and I will take a walk.

"Do you want to take a walk?" he asked Lonny.

"Sure."

"But wait, Carl," the old man said as Carl started toward the door. "Joe's family is coming over here tomorrow after the service. Would you like to come over and meet them? We should be here by three-thirty."

Carl did not want to meet Joe's family, but he knew that it would be harder on the old man.

"Of course," he said. "Robert said something about it. Can I bring anything?"

"Nothing, thanks."

"Well, let me know if you change your mind," Carl said. "Where are you sleeping tonight?" he asked Lonny.

"Beats me."

"On the beach?" Mildred said.

Everyone smiled a little and the old man noticed that Mildred looked tired, and thin in her face.

"Then I'm off," Carl said. He went to the door. "If I don't stop by tonight after work I'll stop by in the morning. So long everybody."

They all said good-bye to Carl, and he closed the door behind him and walked across the deck and out through the gate. He closed the gate and did not ring the bell.

"We have to be going too," Mildred said.

"Why don't you make yourself useful and put that away," she told Lonny, indicating the pan that Carl had left. Lonny got up and put it in the refrigerator.

The old man was looking out the window at the sky.

"It's going to rain before midnight."

"I hope it doesn't rain tomorrow," Elizabeth said, and the old man thought that it did not make any difference but he did not say that.

"Do you want us to come over in the morning for anything?" Mildred asked.

"No, just come in the afternoon."

Elizabeth got up and picked up their basket and Mildred got up, and they went to the door with the old man. Mildred held his hand.

"Remember, a lot of people love you."

The old man nodded and his eyes blurred a little but he did not allow them to go any further. Does Mildred know about the sea he thought. Maybe she's even considered it. He felt a little sad for Mildred now too.

The women said good-bye and left, and the old man and Lonny were alone.

"I'll do the dishes," Lonny said.

"Dishes? Just leave them."

"No," Lonny said. "Somebody's got to do them sometime, so it might as well be me now. I'll just take a couple of minutes and then we can go on your walk."

The old man sat at the table and Lonny washed the dishes. While he did so, he did not think about much except washing dishes. Soon he was done.

"You still want to go on that walk?" he asked.

"Yes, if you do," the old man answered.

"Let's go," Lonny said, and Lonny and the old man walked outside through the door in the kitchen. The sky was gray. They could see the bottoms of clouds rushing past. The air was warm, warm and moist with salt spray.

Lonny held the gate open for the old man.

"Which way?"

"Let's walk on the beach," the old man said, and Lonny said, "If it suits you it suits me," and they walked a little way on the boardwalk toward the center of town and then turned and followed a little walk to the top of some steps over the dunes. They did not either of them speak, and they walked down the steps and across the sand to the water. They stood for a minute looking out to sea and the old man inhaled deeply and sighed as he exhaled. He turned west and walked down the beach in the direction of the Sunken Forest and Lonny walked beside him.

"You know," the old man said, "when you die, you really are alone; no one can help. At that moment you are really, truly alone."

"You're alone when you're living too," Lonny said.

The old man thought about that and they walked on. He kicked a shell into the water.

"That's a matter of choice, isn't it," he said.

"Oh, of course you can have people for company. I like company." Lonny laughed. "But you live for yourself, you know. Nobody lives for you."

They walked on and looked down at the sand. After a minute or two the old man said, "What about love?"

"It's like a throat lozenge. It fixes your throat so it doesn't hurt, but it doesn't cure you. Love's like that. It's nice to have, but you've still got to live your life for yourself by yourself. Nobody can eat for you or breathe for you or think for you or bleed for you." Lonny looked at the old man. "You've got to do it for yourself."

"Or die for you," the old man said softly. I stole that, he thought.

135

They walked slowly down the beach and the sky was gray and the ocean was gray from the reflection of the sky and the breeze, which was coming at them from the southwest into their faces, was warm and moist.

"This beach is beautiful," Lonny said.

"Yes, but it won't last forever."

"It's done a good job so far."

"So far," the old man said, "but not forever."

"How do you figure that?"

The old man stopped, picked up some sand, and looked back toward the east. "This sand was carried down from Montauk and the Hamptons by the current, and from here the current takes it and deposits it along Jones Beach and down toward the city."

"How about that," Lonny said, "there's part of the Hamptons in Cherry Grove."

The old man smiled a little in spite of the hovering part of himself. "The trouble is that back in the thirties when some big storms cut inlets into Great South Bay, jetties were built to keep the inlets from refilling with sand. The jetties prevent the sand from the eastern part of Long Island from getting here, but the current still carries this sand away." The old man let the sand sift through his fingers. "Someday there may be nothing left," he said.

He turned and they again walked down the beach toward the west. Lonny thought about Fire Island being washed away and the old man thought about death and dying, and about Joe. He thought about drowning himself in the sea. He thought about grief and fear, too, but he was calm. He turned to Lonny and spoke as they walked.

"There's a tribe in Australia called the Warramunga that has an unbelievable way to show grief. When someone is dying everyone in the tribe throws themselves on the person, shrieking and wailing, until all that's visible is a writhing mass of people. While the tribespeople are piled on the body they

136

stab themselves in the head with sharp-pointed sticks, which they usually use to dig up vegetables with, and everyone gets all bloody. Then at least one of the men stands and cuts his thighs so deeply with a knife that he severs the muscles, and he falls to the ground. The women suck the blood from his wounds."

Very little bothered Lonny, but the thought of that did, and as he imagined the scene the old man described he felt a little sick.

"That's uncivilized," he said.

"Well, maybe," the old man answered, "but it is a way of expressing grief."

Lonny stopped and the old man stopped beside him. Behind them their footprints stretched out in two lines on the sand.

"You're not going to do anything like that?" Lonny asked.

"No. I'm a little short on pointed sticks, and I like to walk." The old man smiled and he knew he was going to join the sea.

"That tribe?" Lonny said.

"The Warramunga."

"Ya, that one. What do they do with the body when they're finished writhing and wailing?"

"Oh, they just leave it in a tree someplace and go away."

"You certainly do know some strange things," Lonny said as they started walking again. They had passed the end of Cherry Grove and were walking toward Sailors' Haven, the national park, and beyond it the Sunken Forest.

"Do you want to walk through the woods?" the old man asked.

"Sure. Just point me away from the poison ivy."

"I think I can handle that," the old man said, and they walked on. The old man was glad to have Lonny with him and he did not feel so alone. He was not able to stop thinking about death, so he stopped trying to stop thinking about death and his mind ran with grim, somber thoughts.

Lonny was remembering the case of poison ivy he had gotten at the beginning of the summer.

They saw a starfish stranded on the sand. Lonny picked it up and turned it over and watched the hundreds of tiny translucent tentacles reach out and move. One of the starfish's arms had been broken or bitten off, but it was regrowing.

"Wouldn't it be nice if we could do that," Lonny said to the old man. He touched the shorter arm with his other hand.

The old man did not answer. He remembered walking on the beach with Joe on Wednesday, and he remembered Joe picking up starfish and throwing them into the water. He thought again about how Joe would never again enjoy the pleasure of a vigorous swim or of a walk on the beach in sultry air under a gray sky, and the sadness came rushing close to him and part of him watched himself and Lonny walk on the beach. The old man struggled for a few moments but he did not lose control, and they walked on. Lonny threw the starfish as far out in the water as he could and the old man watched it arc up and then down but he could not see it enter the water because it fell into a trough between two waves.

"Have you ever tasted rice wine?" the old man asked.

"I don't think so." Lonny picked up a shell and threw it out into the water. "What's it like?"

"Vile," the old man said, "at least the homemade stuff is. It's made all over Southeast Asia. The natives take rice, wash it, boil it, and then roll it into balls and put it into large jars. They seal the jars and leave them in the sun for a while, and the rice ferments and creates a foul-tasting liquid. When the jars are opened the rice is compressed and the liquid is strained off. The result is really awful."

"How do you know all this crap, anyway?" Lonny pointed down the beach to the steps that led over the dunes

138

and through the Sunken Forest and the two of them angled up away from the water.

"I was in Indonesia once."

"Did you actually drink that stuff?"

"Yes, and I was sick for two days."

"I'll bet. I'd bring my own bottle, thank you."

They reached the steps, and the old man noticed that the sea rocket blossoms had fallen off and that the plant's leaves were limp. They climbed the steps together and Lonny bounced on the balls of his feet.

"There's a tribe in Borneo—" the old man started.

They topped the steps and started down the walk that led across the depression behind the dunes and then up over the hill and down into the woods.

"If this is going to be gross, I'd rather not hear it," Lonny said.

"Yes, I guess it is," the old man answered, and they walked on quietly. Lonny did not think about much and the old man thought about a tribe in Borneo that ferments their dead like rice. When someone dies the body is sealed in a wine-making jar and fermented. The liquid that accumulates is drained off through a hole in the bottom of the jar, and eventually only the bones are left. The bones are then removed from the jar, cleaned, and stored on a shelf.

The old man began to think about cremation but the pictures were too horrible so he thought about joining the sea and although he knew it would not be easy it was a calming thought. Then he allowed himself to think freely and vividly about the cremation the next day while always thinking too of the sea, and his mind ran with images of bright flames and moving waves.

The old man and Lonny followed the walk up and down until they came to the place where it widened out into a rest area. The dead gull was still there, just off the deck into the

139

woods. They stood at the rail and looked down at it. Most of its body was gone; only a shell of bones and feathers remained. Its wings were spread at an unnatural angle.

"Poor thing," Lonny said.

The old man was quiet. Lonny took his arm and led him back to the walk and they walked on through the woods and smelled the greensmell of the bayberry. The old man was happy for Lonny's company and after a while he started to talk again.

"Ever heard of Alexander the Great?"

"Wasn't he Greek or Roman or something?"

"Macedonian."

The old man stopped and pulled some leaves from a bayberry bush. He smelled them and then held them up for Lonny to smell.

"Macedonian. Sounds like the name of a large, extinct animal," Lonny said. "You know, like they found frozen in Alaska or Siberia or someplace."

The old man laughed and the ever-present sadness retreated a little, and he began to find Lonny's vitality and irreverence comforting.

"What'd he do that was so great?" Lonny asked. They had emerged from the forest now and were descending into the hollow behind the dunes.

"He managed to capture most of the world when he was still in his twenties."

"By himself?"

"No, he had a great army. Although many of his soldiers were old men who had fought under his father, and he was very young to lead an army, he managed to convince his men to endure almost unbelievable hardships for him."

Lonny did not speak, and they climbed the steps to the top of the dunes and started down toward the sea.

"One of the cities he conquered was named Tyre," the old man said.

140

"Ya?"

"It was a city on Alexander's route to Egypt, and—"

"Egypt," Lonny interrupted. "He did get around, didn't he?"

"Yes, he sure did. And unfortunately for Tyre, Alexander decided he could not leave it unconquered behind him. The city covered an island about a half mile out in the Mediterranean and it was surrounded by a wall one hundred and fifty feet tall. It really was a difficult strategic problem for Alexander. Back then the only ways to break down a city's walls were to ram them with battering rams or catapult boulders at them or dig a tunnel under them so they would collapse. Since the city was on an island his men couldn't get close enough to do any of those things."

"I wouldn't want to be one of the men digging a tunnel that was meant to collapse," Lonny said.

"Me either."

The old man was quiet, thinking about Joe and his red-brown hair and about Alexander.

"So what happened to the city?" Lonny asked.

"Well, before he took any aggressive action he sent ambassadors to negotiate a peaceful surrender, and the Tyreans killed them and threw them off the wall into the sea in view of Alexander and his men. Then Alexander started building a causeway out toward the city."

"A road?"

"Well, something like one I guess. It was made mostly from logs. He intended to use it as a platform to support his siege towers and catapults."

The two of them, the old man and Lonny, walked down the beach and for a while Lonny concentrated on the old man's story and for a while the old man saw Tyre and Alexander and Alexander's army, and his sadness retreated.

"The Tyreans were pretty smart too," the old man continued. "They filled a ship with inflammable material and

141

sailed it toward the end of Alexander's causeway where the siege towers were. When they got close enough they set the ship on fire and jumped overboard. The causeway was destroyed, and it had taken months to build."

"I'll bet that poor Alexander just cursed a blue streak."

"Maybe, but it was then that he began to prove that he was not only an impetuous youth but that he was also a brilliant general. He built a bigger causeway for his siege towers and he also lashed two ships together and used them to support a battering ram. Then the Tyreans defended themselves by throwing hot sand down on the ships. The sand got inside the soldiers' armor and burned them horribly."

"Boy," Lonny said, "if anyone dumped hot sand on me I'd be plenty pissed."

"Well, they probably were, but they continued to fight."

"How long did this go on?"

"Months and months. Finally, using a combination of ships and battering rams and catapults and archers and infantry, Alexander was successful."

"What happened to Tyre?" Lonny asked.

The old man looked down the beach and tried to imagine a line of crosses. "It was destroyed," he said. "Most of the citizens were either enslaved or killed. Almost two thousand men were crucified along the shore."

"God," Lonny said.

They could see the house now and they walked toward it quietly. The old man tried to imagine what he would have done at Tyre if he had been Alexander and he wanted to tell Joe that Alexander had been a great general and a great man, and he was sad.

When they reached the steps over the dunes Lonny held back and allowed the old man to climb them ahead of him. The old man stopped at the top of the boardwalk and Lonny came up beside him, and they walked toward the old man's house. High overhead the clouds moved by in a solid, gray mass.

"What are you going to do now?" Lonny asked as they came to the gate in front of the house. Beside the gate a single rose blew in the breeze that had come up stronger while they had been walking, and the old man touched the rose gently.

"I've got to rest," he answered, and too, he wanted to be alone to think about the sea and the comfort it would give him.

"OK," Lonny said. "I think I'll go see Carl for a while. I'll come back later."

Lonny patted one of the branches of the stunted pitch pines that grew near the gate, and he pulled the leather cord that was attached to the clapper of the bell.

"Carl's probably still sleeping," the old man said.

"Not for long."

Lonny smiled broadly and then the old man smiled too.

"Would you like to come back for dinner?" he asked. "There's certainly enough food."

"Sure. What time?"

"Maybe around seven?" the old man said.

"I'll be here," Lonny told him. "Now you go take a good nap. You look terrible."

The old man smiled thinly and said that yes he would take a nap and Lonny said he would be back, and the old man went in through the gate and toward the house. Lonny rang the bell again and walked away, toward Carl's house.

The old man went in through the kitchen and continued into the large room that faced the sea. Part of him thought about how tired he was and the part that had before rippled and flowed on beneath the surface now stumbled about searching for a focus. He realized that he had a headache, and he stroked one of the bird of paradise flowers before going into the bathroom for aspirin. He ran a glass of water at the kitchen sink and as he took the pills he noticed, through the window over the sink, that the light outside was a strange, diffuse yellow, and he thought that the cloud layer had thinned but still he knew that eventually it would rain.

You need a rest, he told himself firmly, and he took himself into the front room and up the steps to the loft. He undressed completely, folded his clothes and put them on the top of his dresser, and lay down. He lay on his back and watched the bottoms of the clouds move by and listened to the sea. The loft was filled with the strange yellow light.

The old man sank through levels of consciousness and that part of him that had hovered and analyzed and commented and the part that had moved and remembered and the changing foundation of sadness all collapsed, and the old man fell into sleep. At first he did not dream, but even in his exhaustion he was not free from the wash of the sea, and the sound brought with it a picture of dark water and he could see a figure swimming near the horizon but he could not see if it was Joe. He entered the water and dove through the surf and swam toward the distant swimmer, but the swimmer swam steadily out to sea and although the old man called, the swimmer did not stop or slow and the old man swam further and further from the shore until in his dream he felt like he could not go on.

He turned back and saw that the shore was lined with stunted trees and bushes for as far as he could see, pines and roses he thought, and he swam toward them to investigate. As he drew closer the trees grew taller and thinner and gradually they took the shape of crosses and in his dream the old man was filled with dread. He pulled for the shore and the crosses grew and he began to notice thickets of roses at their bases. The crosses continued to grow and finally he was on the beach and crosses towered over him and extended in a line as far as he could see in each direction, and at the base of each was a cluster of salt-spray roses. He thought that Alexander must be

144

near and in his sleep the old man walked inland and searched for the young Alexander and gradually he forgot about the crosses, and the crosses and the roses diffused into a yellow mist and he forgot whom he was searching for and as, in his sleep, he tried to remember, the image of a tanned young man with long red-brown hair that blew about his face in the wind came to the old man, and he searched for Joe and did not find him.

While the old man slept the clouds came lower and the yellow light that sometimes comes before a summer storm muted and darkened, and when he awoke it was heavily overcast. He could see the bottoms of the clouds moving more rapidly than when he had gone to sleep, and he knew that with the front, rain would come, although he did not expect it for a few hours. He got up and went to the windows and looked out on the sea. The water was dark and the waves moved and broke in disorder, confused by the winds and the currents.

The old man felt less tired now, and he stood by the window and thought about his dream. In it, the search for Joe at the end had not been accompanied by dread and anxiety, but by gentle melancholy, and now the old man's thoughts were tender, although behind them there was the fear of what he knew he was going to do.

He decided to go for a swim before Lonny came for dinner, and he put on a pair of trunks, climbed slowly down to the room below, took a towel from a closet in the room under the loft, and went outside. He walked down the steps to the sand and left his towel up by the dunes. There were a few people walking on the beach but no one was in the water. The old man walked a few feet into the ocean and wet his chest and arms with his hands. The breeze made him cold, so he waded out into the water until it was over his knees and then he dove through the surf.

The longshore current was strong, and as the old man

swam out the current carried him along the beach. He swam against it, trying to stay even with his towel, and part of him observed that although he could swim efficiently in calm water because of his years of practice he no longer had the strength to fight against the sea. I'm old he thought and I have had a fine life and now it's time. For a few seconds he quickly thought that perhaps Joe's accident might have elements of good in it, but part of him was revolted that he had thought it and then the sadness that had stayed away since he had awakened from his nap returned, and he felt his little strength in the water fade.

He swam for shore, but he no longer fought the current and when he could stand in the water he was far down the beach from his towel. Instead of standing and then immediately walking out he stood in thought for a minute and lost his footing as a wave hit his back hard. He went down and he scraped his arm on something in the sand. It stung smartly when he pulled himself out of the water and walked up onto the beach. He was cold and he walked quickly back toward his towel. He was breathing hard and he told himself that yes he was old enough.

When the old man came to his towel he wrapped it over his shoulders and around him and walked quickly back to the house. Inside, he went into the bathroom and poured alcohol on the scrape on his arm and shook his head at the sting, and he started the shower running hot and closed the bathroom door. He went into the kitchen and made a mug of tea. This time he did not use one of the cat mugs but a plain plastic one that carried no memories. He took a sip of tea and carried the mug with him into the bathroom. The room was filled with steam. He set the mug on the sink, adjusted the temperature of the water, and stepped into the shower. And the sadness for Joe was always there, and too the remembering, but now, too, part of him thought about the next day and about the end of the next day.

He shampooed his hair. Maybe I should shave my head he thought and part of him was amused at the thought of himself with a shaved head, and also part of him thought that Joe's father would probably think that a shaved head had something to do with homosexuality. The old man stood under the shower until he was thoroughly warm and after he shut the water off he reached around for his mug of tea before he stepped out. The tea smelled of sweet oranges and cinnamon and cloves and part of the old man reflected that it had been Joe's favorite tea and that Joe would never again experience a rough swim and the cold of the wind on his wet skin followed by a hot shower and a mug of fragrant tea, and the old man was then very sad.

When he had dried himself he wrapped himself in his towel and carried his tea up to the loft. You're in mourning, the hovering part, which was always there, said, wear something dark. The old man dressed in white pants and a light blue shirt and while he dressed he sipped his tea and he looked out at the ocean. A little more than twenty-four hours he thought that's all. The time will pass quickly, the hovering part said, and he thought that was fine, and he thought that maybe he would not spend the entire evening at home with Lonny but would go to the restaurant where there would be noise and light and friends, and he said to himself, I think you're afraid, Old Man, and he knew that he was.

He finished dressing and he took the rest of the tea, cool now, down to the kitchen to wait for Lonny. Too bad about all that food he thought, but the hovering part told him that it would be used tomorrow and that anyway such things were no longer important. He sat and he waited and he drank cool tea, and he remembered, and he wanted the time to pass.

He was thinking about swimming with Joe when the bell rang, and he turned toward the windows and watched Lonny walk across the deck toward the house. Part of the old man

147

wondered if Lonny would knock, but part of him did not care and Lonny walked in.

"Hi," Lonny said. "You look better. That's a pretty shirt."

"Joe gave it to me."

"Good taste," Lonny said. He opened the refrigerator. "I'm hungry. Want me to fix some dinner?"

"Would you like to eat out?" the old man asked.

"Are you sure you want to do that? You've got a hard day tomorrow."

The hovering part told the old man that he wasn't old enough to be treated gently by a kid, but part of him no longer cared, and he said, "Let's let someone else cook."

Lonny easily agreed and as they started to leave he asked the old man if he thought he needed a sweater and the old man told him a little sharply no, and the old man was sad that it was not Joe who would be going to dinner.

"Was Carl sleeping?" the old man asked as they walked across the deck toward the gate.

"Yes, but like I said, not for long." Lonny rang the bell by the gate as they left.

"So, did you sleep?" he asked the old man.

"Yes, and I dreamed about swimming," the old man said, "so when I got up I went for a swim." The old man did not want to tell Lonny about the rest of his dream.

"Swimming!" Lonny looked at the old man as they walked. "You're crazy. I saw the sea. It's pretty rough."

"It's coming up pretty good," the old man agreed. "But nothing like the other night."

The old man remembered sitting on the steps with Joe and looking at the sea and at the stars and talking about satyrs and about fall, and the memory hurt and the sadness drew closer around him. Soon there won't be any more remembering, the hovering part told him, and the old man thought that would be good.

"How come you swim so much?" Lonny asked. "If I live as long as you have, God willing—" Lonny crossed himself, moving his hand from his abdomen to his head and then from his left to his right "—I'm not going to tire myself out swimming. I'm going to sit on a beach somewhere south and drink gin and tonics."

"I've always liked to swim," the old man said. "When I was a boy I often skipped school to go swimming. I usually got hit for it, but I did it anyway."

Lonny walked lightly on his feet and when he came to a soft board in the walk he jumped on it, but it did not break.

"And I'll bet you went to a one-room school out in the country somewhere and went swimming in a swimming hole that had a tree hanging over the water with a rope on it."

"No," the old man told him. "I swam in a river. In the spring it ran fast and it was so cold it made me ache, but I always went whenever I could."

The old man remembered swimming naked in the river in the spring when the grass beside the bank was still a tender green and the jack-in-the-pulpits that grew in the damp ground near the river were just coming up and when the ferns were just unrolling and soft to touch and good to eat, when the trout were still hungry from the winter and could be seen waving in one place against the current. He remembered swimming in the heat of the summer, when the ferns were high and tough and bitter and the jack-in-the-pulpits had gone to red berries and the river flowed slowly and the water was warm and the grass tall and dark green with rough, sharp-edged blades, when the trout hid under rocks or in the hollows the spring currents had cut into the overhanging banks. And he remembered swimming in the fall, when the corn in the fields was brown and the air cool and sweet and the sky deep blue. In those days called Indian summer the old man, then a very young man, could seldom be found at school. Instead, he

149

went to the river and swam and dried himself in the sun and sat on the bank writing in his notebook.

They had almost reached the restaurant while the old man was remembering, and the hovering part noticed that now he was remembering a time before Joe.

"Penny for your thoughts," Lonny said.

"Oh I was just thinking about your question—why I like to swim so much. I think that it was because when I was very young swimming got me away from school and away from the house. When I went to the river I could be alone. I guess I daydreamed a lot."

Part of the old man asked why he was telling the kid this, but part observed that a decision had been made and that Lonny made no difference at all: He could talk to Lonny or not; it was the same.

"Well, you should be careful swimming alone," Lonny told him. They were at the restaurant now. The old man did not go in through the disco but walked down a short board-walk that ran outside the disco to a door near the dining room. The door was open and when they walked in Lonny looked out into the disco but he did not go in. The old man and Lonny waved at Carl, who was behind the inside bar, but they did not go to speak with him.

Robert came up to them. "Are you eating here?" he asked the old man. He was surprised to see him at the restaurant.

"If you'll have us," the old man said.

"You know we've always room for you," Robert told him, and he led the old man and Lonny toward the back himself instead of turning them over to the young man who was his assistant.

"I stopped over this afternoon, but no one was there," Robert said.

"Lonny and I went for a walk," the old man told him.

"That's nice," Robert said. "It's good for you to get out."

The hovering part of the old man tried to decide if he was

150

acting normally, and part of the old man nodded to some people he knew but did not want to talk to.

Robert showed them to a large, round table in a back corner, and he put down two menus and picked up two of the four place settings from the table.

"It will be nice and quiet back here and nobody will bother you," he said. "Now eat a good dinner and I'll talk to you before you leave." Robert walked back toward the front and the old man watched him go.

"I'm starved," Lonny said. He and the old man picked up their menus and talked about what they would eat and the old man said he would drink wine but nothing else, and while they were reading and discussing the menus a waiter came and took their order and took the menus away, and they were silent until the waiter came back with a bottle of wine.

"I don't need to taste it," the old man said. "Just pour it please."

"Sure thing."

The waiter filled the old man's glass and then Lonny's and left the bottle near the old man.

"You never did answer me about the school," Lonny said as they sipped their wine and waited for their soup.

"School?"

"You know, the one you went to when you swam in the river. Was it a one-room affair?"

"No, two. Grades one through four were in one room and grades five through eight were in another."

"How'd you ever get anything done?"

The old man looked out into the room without seeing it and thought of times long past.

"I had the same teacher for the fifth through the eighth grades," he remembered. "She was the minister's wife and every day she talked to us about Christian love and charity and kindness. Then she'd beat it into us just to make sure we

151

understood. She believed in punishment and in the American Standard Bible, in that order."

"You mean she hit you?" Lonny tried to imagine the old man as a boy being hit by his teacher, but he could not.

"She sure did," the old man said. "She had a piece of half-inch-thick bird's-eye maple about a foot and a half long and two inches wide." The old man traced the approximate shape on the tablecloth. "If you did poorly in something or if you were rowdy or if you skipped school she'd call you up to the front of the room and beat the palms of your hands with the bird's-eye until they were red."

The waiter brought two bowls of fresh pea soup. It was fragrant with chervil and a touch of saffron, and it tasted faintly of sherry.

"Good stuff," Lonny said.

The old man agreed that it was good.

"That was some school you went to," Lonny said.

"I guess it was," the old man answered. He smiled at a memory. "Every year everyone in the fifth through the eighth grades had to memorize a passage from the Bible to recite at the end of the year."

The old man paused, remembering the work that often had been done to find the shortest acceptable passages.

"Do you still remember any of the stuff you memorized?" Lonny asked.

"Yes, amazingly for an ancient one, I do. I memorized a chapter of Ecclesiastes each year, and then when I was in high school I memorized the rest of it."

The old man remembered a boy—himself—climbing a set of three steps to a narrow stage made from rows of planks laid over sawhorses with a skirt of green cloth hung in front so the sawhorses did not show. The stage was across the front of the classroom and all the desks in the classroom had been removed and replaced with chairs for the parents. Each child, like Oswald, climbed the steps, walked to the center of the stage, and recited his verses. When the child was through the chairman of the Board of Education shook his hand, and the child was promoted to the next grade. Sometimes, when a child stumbled over the words, parents prompted from the audience.

Occasionally a child would be overcome with nervousness and prompting did not help. The child's parents would look at each other nervously and try to force the child to go on by the projection of their will over the space separating them, and then the chairman of the Board of Education, a kind old farmer who was also the tax assessor, would hand the child a Bible. The child would fumble with the pages and then read timidly, knowing that the bird's-eye would be waiting when school opened in the fall.

The young Oswald spoke flawlessly though, and now, his face gently illuminated by candlelight, the old man recited again.

What does a man gain by all the toil
    at which he labors under the sun?
A generation goes and a generation comes,
    but the earth remains the same.
The sun rises and the sun goes down,
    and hastens to the place where it rises.
The wind blows to the south,
    and goes round to the north;
round and round goes the wind,
    and on its circuits the wind returns.
All streams run to the sea,
    but the sea is not full;
to the place where the streams flow,
    there they flow again.
All things are full of weariness;
    a man cannot utter it;
the eye is not satisfied with seeing,

nor is the ear filled with hearing.
What has been done is what will be,
    and what has been done is what will be done;
and there is nothing new under the sun.

The old man saw the waiter coming toward them, and he came back from the past.

"God, that's beautiful," Lonny said. The waiter set a tray down near them and took away the soup dishes. "That's really in the Bible?"

"There's a lot of good stuff in there," the old man said as the waiter brought plates of scampi to the table. The scampi smelled of garlic and ginger.

The old man looked away, and he thought about the coming day and part of him also searched for things now long ago. The memories of his youth had softened the edges of his memories of Joe, and gradually everything was coming together, coming to an ending. The old man began to feel a little of the tranquillity that is felt by the extremely old, much older than the old man, who quietly accept life and await death and see little difference between them.

Lonny waved his hand in front of the old man's eyes. "You in there?" he said.

"I guess so," the old man answered, and he turned his attention to Lonny, and although part of him still hovered and looked around the room and commented on everything it saw, it did not interfere as much as it had.

The old man picked up his fork and started to eat his dinner. He realized that it was quite good, and he thought that it did not matter.

"How'd you meet Carl?" he asked, more from politeness than interest.

"On the beach," Lonny said. "I was looking for somebody named Malone, and I met Carl."

"Malone dies," the old man said.

"No he doesn't. I think he becomes a monk. Can't you see him in a hooded robe walking with his hands clasped around a crucifix?"

"*Malone Dies* is the title of a novel by Beckett," the old man said.

Lonny thought about that, but he preferred to think of Malone walking in a stone-paved courtyard with Gregorian chants reverberating in the background.

"How'd you end up staying at Carl's house?" the old man asked, interrupting Lonny's romantically religious visions.

The Gregorian chants faded from Lonny's mind. "We talked for a while and then he invited me to stay with him, so I went back to the hotel and brought my stuff back to his house."

The old man thought clearly for a minute.

"Did you plan that?"

"Kind of," Lonny said.

"I like Carl a lot," the old man said, "and I know that he's kind and easy to take advantage of." His voice became hard. "I want you to take it easy on him when you decide to leave."

"Maybe I won't leave," Lonny said.

The old man thought about that, and part of him told himself not to comment. Talk to Carl he thought, that's one thing I've got to do, but then he thought no, it's not your place.

As they ate they talked quietly. The old man talked about being a boy in rural Pennsylvania and Lonny talked about growing up in Baltimore in the wrong part of town. Always part of the old man thought about the next day and the end of it, and Lonny thought about the dinner. Lonny liked dinners. He liked lunches too, but dinners were better.

Their conversation faltered and then stopped, and the old man was content to think and surround himself with silence. Lonny, however, thought that he should at least keep the old man company in return for the fine dinner, and he searched for a topic.

155

"Did you go to college?" he asked.

"Yes, Syracuse University," the old man told him. He started to think about his years at Syracuse.

"I was in Syracuse last year," Lonny said. "I did a show there."

The old man looked into his wine. "I haven't been there for years. I probably wouldn't recognize it now."

"Probably not," Lonny said. "Did you graduate?"

"Of course. Class of thirty-two."

"It must have been some place back then."

"It wasn't that long ago," the old man said, but he knew that it was. "That was quite a year," he said.

"Ya?"

The old man smiled. "You know, I can even remember who the May Queen was. Dorothy Hatch. What a fox."

Lonny did not look very interested, but the old man went on, remembering as he spoke.

"I was on the swim team. Boy, were we bad. When I was a junior we only won one out of ten meets."

"I thought you were a good swimmer," Lonny said as he tried to pull the tail off a shrimp with his fingers.

"I was, but I never liked competition very much."

"Me either," Lonny said.

"Did you go up to the university when you were there?" the old man asked.

"Ya, I went up to look at the sights, if you know what I mean."

The old man liked to look at young men too, and he smiled and nodded.

"How'd you make it from a little two-room school to Syracuse?" Lonny asked.

"I was lucky to be the oldest," the old man told him. "I was expected to go to college and become a doctor. My brothers were expected to stay home, and they did. Neither of them finished high school."

"So what'd your family think when you didn't become a doctor?"

The waiter approached and the old man motioned with his hand for him to clear the table. The old man waited until he had asked for coffee and Lonny had asked for dessert, and by then Lonny had forgotten his question and the old man did not answer, but he remembered the disappointment, and the later disapproval of his books.

Carl came in from the bar as the old man was drinking his coffee and Lonny was eating his cake.

"I got the rest of the night off," Carl said. He put his hand on the back of the chair across from the old man.

"May I sit down?" he asked.

"Please do," the old man said, and Carl pulled out the chair and sat down.

"Would you like something to drink?" the old man asked.

"No thanks. I just thought I'd see how you're doing. I thought maybe I'd walk you home."

Carl put his elbows on the table and leaned forward, and his face glowed in the candlelight.

"I'm doing fine," the old man said. "Your young friend here has been very kind to listen to an old man's ramblings."

Lonny dipped his head in a mock bow.

"I went swimming this afternoon," the old man said.

"Wasn't it a bit rough?"

"A little, but I didn't fight it."

Part of the old man saw himself sitting with Carl and Lonny at the round table in the corner and it saw the candlelight on Carl's face and a rush of sadness came over the old man, and he wanted to be alone.

"I'm going to go back," he said. "Why don't you two stay here and have a drink on me."

Carl and Lonny looked at each other and agreed, and the old man pantomimed writing in the air for the waiter to see, and the waiter took out his pad and started writing on it.

157

"Don't you want me to stay over?" Lonny asked.

"No, that's all right. You should spend some time with Carl."

Part of the old man observed that he did not really care, that he only wanted to be alone, but part of the old man looked on Lonny with tenderness and looked on Carl with tenderness and protectiveness.

The waiter came with the check, and the old man started to sign it. Then he thought and stopped and took out some bills from his front pocket and handed them to the waiter. When the waiter returned with the change the old man handed him twenty dollars and said "This is for you," and he handed him twenty more dollars and said "This is to pay for whatever these two want to drink." He smiled at Carl and Lonny.

The waiter took an order from them, and they thanked the old man and they made plans to come to the old man's house the next morning. The old man said good-bye quietly and Carl and Lonny said good-bye, and the old man left. He walked through the dining room and at the entrance he turned back to wave, but Carl and Lonny had moved closer to each other and did not look up. The old man turned to go out.

Robert was by his stand-up desk.

"Is it all set for tomorrow?" the old man asked.

"Everything's taken care of," Robert told him. He put his hand on the old man's shoulder and although the old man had wanted to be alone, part of him welcomed the contact, and then he nearly cried.

Robert squeezed his shoulder a little. "Is it all right if I stop over in the morning?" he asked.

The old man nodded and did not speak, and he turned away, and Robert walked beside him to the door.

"Take it easy," Robert told him, and again the old man nodded and did not speak and his eyes filled, and then Robert's eyes filled also. Robert turned back inside quickly so the old man could not see his tears and the old man walked away.

158

As he walked down the boardwalk toward the sea a few big drops of water began to fall from the sky and hit the walk, and the old man felt a tear start down the side of his face and he no longer tried to fight it; even the hovering part gave in to grief. The old man walked toward his house and the rain came and water from the sky ran down his face and water from his eyes ran down his face, and his tears intensified with the rain. When he reached his house he did not go in, but went around the side to the front deck and stood facing the sea. The wind was blowing the rain across the water and onto the land and the old man held the rail and sobbed into the face of the wind and the rain. He sobbed for Joe and for himself, he sobbed for long past disappointments and shames, and he remembered Joe once standing naked in the rain, laughing, and the old man sobbed to hear Joe's laughter and to feel his touch.

He stood holding the rail tightly for a long time and gradually his chest stopped heaving and his tears stopped and only the rain wet his face, and the old man became calm, and he hoped that now the calm would last as long as it had to, and he pulled his long wet hair back from his face and held his fists up and shook them at the sky, and then he enjoyed the storm.

When he began to feel cold he left the rail and went around the house and in through the kitchen door. He left his shoes by the door, and he took off his clothes and hung them over the shower-curtain rod in the bathroom and dried himself thoroughly. The hovering part was still there and it told him he was cold, so he wrapped himself in a towel and went into the kitchen. He poured himself a good dose of scotch and drank it, and then went into the front room and up into the loft. He got into bed quickly. The rain hammered at the sky-lights and tore at the windows, and the old man slept.

In his sleep he could still hear the rain, and then again he faced a stormy sea and rain washed his face and tears fell from a pool of grief, and as he looked out over the water he could see something coming at him from out of the rain and the mist. At first it was indistinguishable, but it came nearer and nearer and the old man in his dream began to be able to make out a double column of figures coming over the waves. The figures drew nearer and grew larger and larger, and the old man knew that it was a procession of Olympian gods but saw that there were two of each one. The procession was led by two immense, terrifying figures of Zeus, and the old man felt the fear of death. The figures advanced and the old man could not run, and he stood helpless, waiting to be crushed, as under the wheels of a juggernaut.

The fear grew, and then, when the gods were almost upon him, the procession split, one column going to his left and the other to his right, and as the old man looked up and down the beach he became aware that the beach was now lined with huge crosses, and even in his dream he remembered dreaming about the crosses before and he went down to find the roses. As he came to the crosses he saw that there was a man hanging on each one, and as he walked to the front of the crosses and turned his back to the sea he saw that the man hanging on the nearest cross was Joe, and he turned and ran down the beach in terror. As the old man passed each cross the man on it was still Joe, and as he ran he saw more and more of the details and he saw that Joe's chest had been eaten away and that his arms were at an unnatural angle.

The old man ran and the crosses stretched endlessly before him and behind him and in the distance they looked like snow fence on the beach, and in his sleep he became exhausted so he turned inland. His feet found the steps leading to the forest and he ran up the steps and down into the hollow behind the dunes and up the hill and down into the forest, and in his dream the heights and depths were exaggerated and the running was hard. He reached the resting place and he stopped, and he saw the dead gull. Now it was larger, man-sized. The old man turned it over and it too was Joe, bloodied and half-eaten.

The old man then screamed in his sleep but did not

awake, and in his dream he collapsed on the deck of the resting place and waited for something horrifying and unknown. As he lay on the deck he gradually became aware that out under the trees a light was glowing roundly, like a soft candle glows in the imagination, and the old man pulled himself toward it and as he did the light rose from the ground and grew brighter and whiter and came toward him.

The old man came to his feet and the light and the old man drew closer and the old man felt the light tell him, walk with me, and the old man started back toward the beach and the light was beside him. They went over the hill and down into the hollow and up over the dunes together and the light was warm and comforting and the walk was easy. When they reached the beach the crosses were gone and the rain had stopped and the sky was clearing and the old man knew that the presence with him wanted him to go home.

The old man walked down the beach bathed in the glow from his companion until they were in front of the old man's house. The light pulled away from the old man toward the sea and held itself between the water and the old man and then, as he stood and faced it, the light closed the distance between them and surrounded him, and the old man felt Joe's naked touch and heard the sound of his laughter and felt his breath on his chest and the old man stood and cried while the light embraced him and gradually his grief was eased away and he came to an immutable calm and warmth, and when the light released him and drew away the calm and the warmth remained, and the old man felt that Joe was with him and he watched without sadness as the light pulled back. The light receded over the water toward the west and as it reached the horizon it filled the sky and the sea with gold, and then it was gone and the old man slept calmly.

While the old man slept the rain slackened and stopped and then came up again, but not as hard, and by early morning it had stopped completely. When the old man awoke he turned from his side onto his back and looked at the sky. It was gray but not dark and the old man knew that the cloud layer was thin and would break up during the day. Today is the day the hovering part told him, and the old man knew that today was the day and he was sad but calm, and at the same time he could feel fear growing under the detached calmness. His sadness was no longer the top of a well of unexpressed grief or a remorse for the end of his own life but was a distant sadness at the constancy of time: The day would go on irresistibly toward its end without pause or compassion. And yet, too, he wanted the time to pass quickly.

Up! part of him told himself, and the old man sat on the edge of the bed, then stood, and then walked to his dresser and wrapped himself in a robe. He went down into the kitchen and measured coffee and water and turned on the coffee maker. The red light in the switch glowed to show that the machine was on. The old man touched the light and it was cool. I've got to eat a good breakfast he thought, today's going to be long, and he went into the bathroom to shower while the coffee maker hissed and dripped in the kitchen.

Standing in the hot spray of the shower he thought about the storm, and he regretted that he would not again experience a summer storm that swept across the island from the sea. I must have looked like an old fool out there shaking my fists at the sky he thought. Well, at least I'll never be senile. He thought about his finances, but not too much. I'll pay some things today and my lawyer can take care of the rest he thought, and the old man was glad that he had named his lawyer a second executor after Joe.

He shut off the water and got out, and when he was dry he put his robe back on and went back to the kitchen. The coffee was done and he poured some into one of the cat mugs and he thought about Joe and missed him, but he knew that when he thought back at the end of the day the day would

162

seem short so he did not begrudge life its last few hours. He made himself a good breakfast and ate it while sitting at the kitchen table in his bathrobe.

While he ate he thought mostly about joining the sea. Join the sea he thought, why don't I call it what it is. Suicide. All the writers who wrote about suicide—Plato, Montaigne, Donne, Camus, and all the rest—they were all wrong. Suicide is not an intellectual decision; it is not a magnificent gesture; it is not a trap suddenly sprung on an unwilling victim. For some of us it's inevitable. I've been on the path since Joe left Wednesday, and from the time Joe met me in New York ten years ago, and before that since the day he decided to take my class, since the time I decided to teach at Yale, and before that when I published my first book, and even before that when I crossed the fields to the woods and walked down the hill and across the marshy lowland to the river to swim and then wrote in my notebook on the bank.

A sadness at the steady passing of time came a little closer, but still the old man was calm and still he wanted time to pass quickly, and he tried not to be afraid. The hovering part was there if he thought about it, but the old man knew his destiny now and there was much to do before the day ended, so he did not now watch himself as carefully. When he finished breakfast he washed his dishes quickly, poured himself more coffee, and went up to the loft to dress. After looking at his clothes he picked tan pants and a green Lacoste shirt, and when he was dressed he took his coffee down to his desk. The vase of flowers was still there from the morning before, and he touched the flowers gently and moved them back to the low glass table along the wall opposite the loft, and he returned to his desk and sat facing the sea. More than an hour had passed since the old man had awoken.

The sea was calmer now, and the tide was on the ebb. The old man watched the sea for a few minutes and wondered how far he would be able to swim. I'll give it a good effort he thought, and he turned his attention to his desk. First he took out the manuscript he had been working on. He had stopped writing the day before in the middle of a paragraph, and after reading all that he had written the day before he finished the paragraph, read it once over, and drew a thick black line across the page under it with his fountain pen. He replaced the manuscript in its folder and put it back in the top drawer.

The old man next took out his checkbook and a few bills. Why bother, the hovering part said, but he paid everything. He put the checks and the bills in envelopes, put stamps on them, and piled the envelopes neatly on the corner of his desk. Time's marching he thought, but he allowed himself to take off his glasses and watch the sea through blurred eyes and he missed the sound of a typewriter. Then he thought about the restaurant, and he put his glasses back on and took out a small pad. He calculated roughly what he owed, added five hundred dollars to it, and wrote a check. He took out a piece of stationery with his name printed on the top of it and wrote ON ACCOUNT in the middle of the sheet. He addressed an envelope, put a stamp on it, and slid it under the pile of other mail.

He was finished then, and he put his pen away and pushed his chair away from the desk. He decided to go out on the deck and read, and he went into the room under the loft for a book. The walls were lined with filled bookshelves and the old man stood in front of them thinking, and then with a smile he took down a Bible and went back into the big room. He took the coffee mug from his desk to the kitchen and went back into the front room and out onto the deck, and more than two hours had passed.

The chairs on the deck were wet, so the old man set the book on the rail and went inside for a towel. When he came back he dried one of the lounge chairs, hung the towel over the rail, and sat down with his Bible. He looked at the sea for a while, and then he opened the Bible to Ecclesiastes. Why read something you know, the hovering part told him, and part of him also was aware that time was passing, and the old man ignored everything and read. He formed the words with his lips and when he reached his favorite passage he read aloud softly:

For everything there is a season,
    and a time for every matter under heaven:
a time to be born, and a time to die;
a time to plant, and a time to pluck up what is planted;
a time to kill, and a time to heal;
a time to break down, and a time to build up;
a time to weep, and a time to laugh;
a time to mourn, and a time to dance;
a time to cast away stones, and a time to gather stones
    together;
a time to embrace, and a time to refrain from embracing;
a time to seek, and a time to lose;
a time to keep, and a time to cast away;
a time to rend, and a time to sew;
a time to keep silent, and a time to speak;
a time to love, and a time to hate;
a time for war, and a time for peace.

The old man stopped then and looked out at the sea and part of him began to run along remembering, but it was not a confused remembering: It was a summing up.

When the bell by the gate rang the old man heard it as if from a distance, and it was an irritation for the old man to have to draw his attention back from where he had been. He got up slowly and walked around the side of the house carrying his Bible.

Robert was at the gate. He was wearing a white caftan and no beads.

"Hi," Robert said. "I just thought I'd come over and see how everything was."

165

"Everything's fine," the old man said, and part of the old man wanted to tell Robert about his plans but he did not.

"Coming in?" he asked.

"For a few minutes, if that's OK."

"Come on in," the old man said.

They walked toward the kitchen door. The old man took down the key and gave it to Robert.

"Here. You might as well take this now."

Robert accepted the key and nodded, and they went inside. The old man put the Bible on the table and started fresh coffee and Robert wandered into the front room. "These flowers are beautiful," he called.

The old man came into the room. "Joe sent them Thursday morning on his way to the city," he said. The old man tried to remember exactly how Joe and he had said good-bye that morning, but he could not.

"Oh, I'm sorry," Robert said. He did not know what else to say.

"I know," the old man answered. "I'd rather have Joe."

Part of the old man was happy that he would never see the bird of paradise flowers turn spotted and brown and then die, but the old man was sad too that he would never again see bird of paradise flowers growing wild under tropical skies where palm branches rustled in the wind.

Robert felt that there was something strange about the old man and he could not understand it.

"I really think you should take someone with you today," he said. "Either Carl or Elizabeth."

"No, I can't. I told Mr. Ross I'd come alone. Besides, no one can change anything." The old man remembered the last funeral he had attended and some of the calm he had built for himself left and some of the sadness returned, and too he felt the time pass.

"Do you mind if I put on some music?" the old man asked.

"No, I'd enjoy it. It sounds like the coffee's done. Would you like me to get you some?"

"A little," the old man answered. "The mug I was using this morning is on the side of the sink. You can just give it a rinse and use that for me."

Robert went into the kitchen and the old man went to get a record from the room under the loft. Something happy, he thought, and he pulled out a record of Mozart's *Jupiter Symphony* and brought it into the front room.

"Do you want anything in your coffee?" Robert called in.

"No thanks. Black," the old man called back. He put the record on the turntable and pushed the switch, and he watched the arm rise, move, and sink slowly to the surface of the record, and he thought there goes three seconds.

Robert brought in the coffee and they sat by the old man's desk in front of the windows looking out on the sea. The old man had wanted to be alone, but now he enjoyed Robert's company. They spoke little and the old man hummed along with the music and as he did he saw a patch of blue sky through the clouds and he smiled because he had been right about the day clearing.

"It's almost ten-thirty," Robert said. "What time do you have to leave?"

"I'm catching the eleven-thirty boat, so I'll probably leave here about quarter after."

The old man began to think about the ferry. The last time he had taken it he had been going to a shopping center on the mainland, as Long Island is called on Fire Island. Joe had been with him, and they had sat on the benches on the top and a crewman warned them that there might be a spray. There was, too. The boat headed into the wind and bucked on the crests of the waves and the wind blew the spray back over them. They did not mind, and Joe caught some of the salty spray with his tongue. The ache and the sadness for Joe came back hard now, and the old man swallowed heavily and part of him felt time slide by and that started to give him an uneasy feeling in his stomach.

The record had stopped and Robert watched the old man silently. When Robert shifted in his chair the old man turned to him slowly.

"I'm sorry," he said. "I was off somewhere. Why don't you put on another record. I'm going up to change."

Robert agreed, and the old man went up to the loft and looked at his clothes. I should wear something dark he thought, but then he thought that's stupid, Joe would think so too, and he changed into a pink shirt but left the tan slacks on. Downstairs, Robert had put on a record of Stravinsky's *Firebird,* and as it began both Robert and the old man remembered a summer when all of the discos on Fire Island had vibrated with the dark, ominous sounds of a disco version of *The Firebird.*

The old man sat on the edge of the bed and he remembered Joe dancing to *The Firebird* while he watched. Joe was shirtless and his sweaty chest shined under the colored strobe lights, and the old man remembered people calling good-bye to Joe and to him as they left the disco and went out into the night, and the old man remembered Joe's laughter as he walked on the boardwalk beside him carrying his shirt in his hand. Then, when he remembered that night, the old man cursed the island and he cursed Joe's father and he cursed the sea and he cursed the gods and cursed his life, and time ran on and not much of his calm remained and his sadness grew.

Robert had looked up at the old man sitting on the bed and had then gone quietly out onto the deck, and it was Robert who went around the house to the side away from the sea when he heard the bell. The old man heard the bell too, but he did not move.

Robert reached the front of the house, his caftan flowing

behind him, as Lonny was starting to open the kitchen door. Carl was with him, and Robert spoke to them both.

"He's up in the loft. I think he needs some time alone. Why don't we go sit in front; we can walk him to the ferry when he goes."

They walked around the side of the house and Carl asked how the old man was doing.

"I don't know," Robert said. "He seems strange. You know how he's usually so sharp and how he always listens when someone talks to him?"

Carl nodded, and Lonny said "Yeah, and he sure talks a lot too," and both Carl and Robert gave Lonny looks whose meaning was immediately clear to him.

"Well," Robert said, "today he doesn't seem like he's all there. He doesn't really listen when you talk to him. He just sits and looks at the ocean."

Lonny sat in the lounge chair that the old man had been using. The canvas chairs were damp so Carl and Robert leaned against the wall. "You know," Lonny said, "I haven't known him as long as you two have—"

"You've known him three days," Robert interrupted.

"As I said, I haven't known him as long as you have, but if I were you I'd be worried that he might do himself in."

"He'd never do anything like that," Carl said. "He's too smart."

"Now I'm not smart," Lonny said, although he thought he was, "but I know that being smart doesn't have anything to do with it. Geniuses commit suicide."

"Name one," Carl said.

"I don't know—Einstein?"

"Wrong," Carl told him, but Robert was thinking about what Lonny had said.

"What makes you think that?" he asked.

"Look at it from his standpoint. He's an old man, and

169

now he's alone when he never thought he would be. And not only that, Joe was body beautiful. Hell, I'd kill myself if I lost Joe."

"Be serious," Carl said.

"He's not alone," Robert said. "He's got us, and Elizabeth and Mildred, and a lot of other people who love him."

"Well, we should keep him company for a while," Lonny said.

"Did you ask him what to do with the money?" Carl asked.

"He wasn't here when I came by this morning, so I haven't had a chance to," Robert said. "I will, or you can if you want."

"How much is it now, anyway?"

"About twelve hundred dollars as of last night, with more promised. Plus Mildred's fifteen hundred."

"I don't care what any of you said, I sent flowers," Lonny told them.

Carl shook his head.

The old man slid the door open from the house. "Morning, guys," he said. He was wearing a blue cotton blazer over his shirt.

"What time is it anyway?"

"Eleven-ten," Robert told him.

The old man felt a little sick at how quickly time had passed, but he was composed and distant.

"We've got to ask you something," Carl said.

"Yes."

"Elizabeth told us not to send flowers, so we've collected some money to give to something in Joe's name."

"You have?" The old man was surprised, and sad.

"Almost everyone who comes into the restaurant asks what they can do," Robert said. "People have given over twelve hundred dollars already, and Mildred, unbelievably,

170

called Carl and told him she would bring a check for fifteen hundred herself."

The old man smiled and he wished that Joe could have known.

"I don't know about the money," he said. "I'll have to ask Joe's father."

Robert thought it should go to something Joe was interested in, but he did not comment.

Time, the old man thought, it's almost time. "Well, I guess it's about the time," he said aloud. "Why don't you wait for me out front. I'll be right out."

The old man went into the house. It looks OK he thought, and he picked up the envelopes from his desk to mail but then decided to do it later and he put them down on Joe's desk. He looked at the flowers and then went into the kitchen and stopped with his hand on the door. Now you've got to do this and you've got to be strong, he thought. No tears.

He opened the door and went out and pulled the door shut behind him and made sure it was locked, and he crossed the deck to where the others were waiting by the gate.

"You have the key?" he asked Robert.

"Yes. I'm sending the food over around three," he added.

"Thanks," the old man said. "You know," he told them all, "you don't have to go to the ferry with me."

"We know," Lonny said, "but we're going to," and he took the old man's hand and led him through the gate. Lonny did not ring the bell.

Lonny and the old man walked ahead and Carl and Robert walked behind, and they went straight toward the bay and then turned west toward the center of town. Carl and Robert talked quietly and the old man pointed out plants and trees to Lonny. The clouds above them were breaking up, and as they walked a line between sunlight and cloud shadow raced across the island and they were caught up in the sunlight. The old

171

man's white hair blew gently about his face in the August breeze. The sunlight warmed him and it calmed him a little, but he was still apprehensive and aware of the passing of time.

They passed the post office and turned toward the bay. The ferry was tied up and there was a small crowd of people on the dock. As the old man walked out to the boat he realized that he knew everyone there, and then one of the people came to him and shook his hand and told the old man how sorry he was, and then everyone gathered around the old man and some shook his hand and some embraced him and everyone had kind words, and the old man wiped his eyes with the back of his hand.

A crewman told him that it was time to go.

"Don't worry about anything," Robert told him, "we'll take care of everything."

"I'll be on the three o'clock boat," the old man said. He looked around at the people on the dock. "I wish I could tell Joe—" He paused, and then stopped and looked away.

Lonny took the old man's hand and squeezed it, and the old man turned and boarded and climbed to the top of the ferry and sat in the bow. The crewmen threw off the lines and the ferry arched away across Great South Bay. The people on the dock slowly drifted away.

The ferry was running in front of the wind, and the spray was not blown back over the top but away to the sides. The old man sat with his hands on his lap and felt the time pass and wished now that it would pass more quickly. When the ferry reached the channel the old man looked at the motel where Joe's family was staying and he did not see anyone he recognized. Ten minutes he thought, five to the dock and five to walk down the street, and he turned and looked ahead and felt his apprehension in his stomach.

The Rosses were on a covered patio outside the motel that faced out across the bay toward Fire Island. Mr. Ross stood

172

and watched as the ferry came in from the bay, and he watched as the captain cut the throttles and the boat slowed and settled in the water and proceeded past the motel and up the channel. His son stood beside him, and his wife sat in a chair a few feet away.

Mr. Ross was heavy and fleshy, but his fat disguised the fact that he was strong and agile. He liked games and contests and success. It was a sport of his to casually ask new, young employees in the company he owned for a game of handball in the winter or a game of tennis in the summer. The young men would always agree because Mr. Ross was the owner, and after they agreed they always thought about whether they should let Mr. Ross win or play a good game and beat him. Such thoughts were unnecessary; Mr. Ross usually ran the employee around the court until he almost dropped, and then threw him a towel and said, "Better luck next time," and then laughed.

As Mr. Ross's fat disguised a strong body, so his language disguised a strong mind. He often spoke coarsely and meanly, but he did not always believe what he said. While he and his son watched the ferry pass he said, "I'll bet that whole boat's full of queers. If I had a bazooka I could sink the damned thing and do the world a favor."

His son did not answer.

"Isn't that right, Scott?" Mr. Ross said.

"I guess so."

Mr. Ross did not like failures, and even before he had known exactly what Joe was he had considered himself a failure because of Joe. He did not make any mistakes with his second son; under his father's guidance Scott had from an early age not only been an excellent student but had also excelled at every sport he tried. And his father had done more for him too: When Scott was sixteen his father gave him a new car and made sure that he had enough money to do as he wanted. Mr. Ross assumed that anyone as handsome as Scott with both a

173

car and money would have no trouble attracting girls, and he was correct.

The day he gave Scott the car Mr. Ross told him to keep his grades up, and the next marking period after that day Scott's grades dropped significantly. Mr. Ross did not take the car away; he methodically beat Scott with his fists until both eyes were black and his nose bloodied. There was no more trouble about the car, and Mr. Ross told Scott to learn some boxing so he could protect himself.

Mrs. Ross heard her husband's comment about the ferry, and she stood up and walked over to him.

"Now Joe, take it easy. It's going to be hard enough for Mr. Stevenson as it is," she said.

"I know, Jan, but I don't like to think about Joe being one of those creatures on that boat."

"You be polite when he gets here," Mrs. Ross told her husband firmly. "And you too," she said to Scott.

The men agreed to be polite, and Mr. Ross said that he thought there was time for a quick Bloody Mary.

"Anyone else?" he asked.

His wife and son answered no, and he went inside.

This is going to be one goddamned bastard of a day he thought while he walked to the bar. "A Bloody Mary and step on it," he said to the bartender. The bartender made the drink and Mr. Ross handed him a five-dollar bill. "Keep the change," he said, and he went back outside.

Scott and his mother were both sitting when Mr. Ross returned, and they both turned as he approached.

"Oh, it's you," Mrs. Ross said. "He should be here any minute."

Mr. Ross nodded, and he stepped off the patio and walked across the grass to the water. Fire Island was a long, thin line across the bay and he stared at it while he held his drink in front of him.

The old man walked up the sidewalk and into the motel,

174

and his stomach felt bad. I wonder if I'm getting an ulcer he thought, and then he thought well I've got the cure, and he went to the desk and asked for Joseph Ross and the clerk said that he was outside and he pointed to the patio.

The old man went outside and walked to the woman sitting in the chair.

"Mrs. Ross?" he said.

"Oh my God, I didn't see you," she said. She stood up. "Hello Mr. Stevenson," she said. She held out her hand.

"Oswald," he said as he shook her hand. I know she's in her fifties but she doesn't even look forty he thought. Mrs. Ross was trim and well groomed; she wore a loose-fitting light blue dress.

"I'm sorry about your son, Mrs. Ross," the old man said, and he thought my son too.

"Please call me Janet," she said. "I'm sorry too; I'm sure it was as big a shock to you as it was to us."

Scott had stood up at the old man's right, and now the old man turned to him. "You look so much like your brother did," he said. "You've certainly grown up since the last time I saw you."

"We all do," Scott said.

Mr. Ross turned and saw them standing together, and he gulped some of his drink and put the glass down on the grass and came across the lawn toward them. The old man looked steadily at him, and the old man was afraid. He waited for Mr. Ross to speak first.

"Hello Mr. Stevenson." Mr. Ross held out his hand. "We don't seem to meet at very pleasant times, do we?"

"Please call me Oswald," the old man said. The name felt a little strange to him. The men watched each other silently until the old man spoke again.

"I guess I don't know what to say to you. I'm sorry for you about Joe. A lot of people will miss him. He made friends wherever he went."

175

A wave of grief and remorse passed over Mr. Ross. "We all die sometime," he said.

Hardhearted bastard the old man thought, and he forced himself to think of the sea and some of his calm returned.

"Shouldn't we be going?" he asked, and Mr. Ross said yes they should and they all went through the motel and out into the parking lot.

"This is it," Mr. Ross said. He pointed to a white, rented Cadillac.

"I'll get in back," the old man said.

"Why don't you ride up front with me and let the women and boys ride in the back," Mr. Ross said. Scott looked hard at his father, and the old man quietly got into the front and thought that time was not passing quickly enough.

"I drove over this morning and took care of the rest of the details," Mr. Ross told him. "I managed to get a copy of the autopsy report too. You can see it if you want."

"No," the old man said, and he started to again think of the crash.

"I'm going to sue the kid who was driving. Did you know they found marijuana in the van?"

The old man said no, he did not know, and he did not care either but he did not say that.

"How do you like Northwestern?" the old man asked back over his shoulder.

"I like it," Scott said. "It's a pretty good school."

They came to a traffic light and Mr. Ross blew the horn in frustration as the light turned red.

"We'll never make it by twelve-thirty," he said.

Joe will wait the old man thought. "What are you studying?" he asked Scott, although he already knew.

"Just literature."

"And it's damned useless, too," Mr. Ross added.

"Now Joe,"—the old man was uncomfortable to hear the

176

name—"you know that you were an English major in college too," Mrs. Ross said.

Mr. Ross smiled a little and did not answer, and as they drove the old man talked to Scott about literature and waited for the day to end, and he did not see the grief in Joe's father because he was not looking for it.

"Well, this is it," Mr. Ross said as he turned into a driveway. The building was made of brick. The main part of the building was two stories tall of Georgian design with white columns in front, and there was a one-story, windowless, flat-roofed extension from one side. The old man got out of the car and held the door open for Mrs. Ross, and they walked on the sidewalk from the side of the building around to the front and then up the steps.

A young man in a dark suit greeted them inside and spoke to Mr. Ross by name. They stood for a moment, uncertain, and the young man told them they could go in whenever they wanted to. The young man escorted them to the door of a small chapel. "Father Cairns will be in in a few minutes," he said, and he left and closed the door gently behind him.

The old man looked at the front of the room quickly and did not look at it again. He sat in the back with his eyes closed, and he waited. Joe's family went to the front. His parents sat in the second row and Scott sat directly behind them. There were only two arrangements of flowers in the room, but they perfumed the air and they made the old man wish for clean sea air, and the passing of time slowed.

A door opened in the back and the priest came out. He crossed the room to a lectern and placed a book on it and smiled at the people in the room. Then he opened the book and began to read, and part of the old man listened and again part of him watched and remembered.

177

I am Resurrection and
I am Life, says the Lord.
Whoever has faith in me
shall have life, even
though he die. And every-
one who has life, and has
committed himself to me
in faith, shall not die
forever. As for me, I
know that my Redeemer
lives and that at the
last he shall stand upon
the earth. After my
awakening he will raise
me up; and in my body I
shall see God. I myself
shall see, and my eyes
behold him who is my
friend and not a stranger.
For none of us becomes his
own master when he dies.
For if we have life, we
are alive in the Lord,
and if we die, we die in
the Lord. So, then, whether
we live or die, we are
the Lord's possession.
Happy from now on are
those who die in the Lord!
So it is, says the spirit,
for they rest from their
labors. The Lord be with
you.
And also with you.
Let us pray. O God of

Joe wouldn't have liked this.
He always said that the best
thing Gertrude Stein said was
when a Jew's dead he's dead.
Joe said he should have been
born Jewish. Remember once
he said he'd convert to piss
off his father, then he could
get him on two counts and if
he could turn black there'd
be three—I wonder if they
spray flower scent in here
those few flowers couldn't
have that much scent in them.
Wonder who they're from Joe's
father said no flowers—what
is wrong with that man he
treats his wife like a chattel
sounds like cattle—that drive
through Pennsylvania when
Joe insisted we stop at a farm
so he could milk a cow; he went
to the door and asked and the
woman he spoke to thought
he was going to rob her so
he offered her five dollars
and she sent him out to the
barn—possession of the Lord
Joe used to say he was proud
of not belonging to anyone
not even me he said when a
Jew's dead he's dead—one—two—
that's two seconds less.
And also with you.
Joe wouldn't have liked all

178

grace and glory, we
remember before you this
day our brother Joe. We
thank you for giving him
to us, his family and
friends, to know and to
love as a companion on
our earthly pilgrimage.
In your boundless com-
passion, console us who
mourn. Give us faith to
see in death the gate of
eternal life, so that in
quiet confidence we may
continue our course on
earth, until, by your call,
we are reunited with those
who have gone before;
through Jesus Christ our
Lord.
Amen
I will read first from
Job. Have pity on me,
have pity on me, O you my
friends, for the hand of
God has touched me! Why
do you, like God, pursue
me? Why are you not
satisfied with my flesh? Oh
that my words were written!
Oh that they were inscribed
in a book! Oh that with
an iron pen and lead they
were graven in the rock
forever! I know that my

this praying—he went to that
white party dressed as an
angel the wings were a hit.
Brother Joe lover Joe son Joe
too his father may be a
successful businessman but I was
right when I called him a
primitive Scott'll be the
same someday. We lost the best
one the sea will be consolation
enough leave faith to those
who need it Joe was my faith.
Socrates believed in eternal
life he wanted to see Homer when
Joe's dead he's dead his life
line ended and that's all.
Robert should try wearing
clerical robes more interesting
than those caftans they come
in nice colors where—
Amen
Amen the end, almost, a few more
hours. No pity don't want
pity rather have people say
the old man must have really
loved him—he read this before,
different translation—Joe in
my life was like being touched
by God, so alive so vital he had
a presence. Flesh was nice too.
Why did he do it? I was old and
he young and beautiful, I never
understood—I'm here aren't I,
he'd say. There's a way
to get immortality: have one

179

Redeemer lives, and at
last he will stand upon
the earth; and after my
skin has been thus
destroyed, then from my
flesh I shall see God,
whom I shall see on my
side, and my eyes shall
behold, and not another.
My heart faints within
me!
And now I will read from
Revelation. And I saw
the holy city, new Jerusalem,
coming down out of heaven
from God, prepared
as a bride adorned
for her husband; and I
heard a great voice from
the throne saying "behold,
the dwelling of God is
with men. He will dwell
with them, and they shall
be his people, and God himself will be with them;
he will wipe away every
tear from their eyes,
and death shall be no
more, neither shall there
be mourning nor crying nor
pain any more, for the
former things have passed
away.
Our father which art in
heaven, Hallowed be thy

of my books engraved in stone
somewhere. Funny, next week
when the news is out my books
will all sell, new printings
probably, maybe a collected
edition—God, Joe's letters
I wanted them to be destroyed and
what if they're published, but
I won't care then. I don't
think I'd want to see God. My
heart would faint too. The
author of Revelation—was it
John?—must have been on drugs,
like Coleridge. In Xanadu
did Kublai Khan a stately
pleasure dome decree: where
Alph, the sacred river, ran
through caverns measureless
to man down to a sunless sea.
Wouldn't like a sunless sea—
cold, lifeless. If we are our-
selves God does God live with us—
that implies two what if
there is only one, but sometimes I watch myself think,
maybe that's where God is,
in our mind. No tears don't
want any tears once was enough.
Nice idea no more death but wasn't
it Gertrude who said that if
everyone lived forever there
wouldn't be enough room. Soon
I'll be a former thing and—
Our father which art in
heaven, Hallowed be thy

name. Thy kingdom come.
Thy will be done in earth
as it is in heaven. Give
us this day our daily bread.
And forgive us our debts,
as we forgive our debtors.
And lead us not into
temptation, but deliver
us from evil: for thine
is the kingdom, and the
power, and the glory,
forever. Amen.
Father of us all, we
pray to you for Joe, and
for all those whom we love
but see no longer. Grant
to them eternal rest. Let
light perpetual shine upon
them. May his soul and the
souls of all the departed,
through the mercy of God,
rest in peace. *Amen.*

name. Thy kingdom come.
Thy will be done in earth
as it is in heaven. Give
us this day our daily bread.
And forgive us our trespasses,
as we forgive those who trespass—
And lead us not into
temptation, but deliver
us from evil: for thine
is the kingdom, and the
power, and the glory,
forever and ever. Amen.
Almost over now I want to
leave quickly. Joe doesn't
need prayers—worry about
the living not the dead.
They've got eternal rest
anyway, rest like anesthesia.
Joe would like that part about
the light beautiful light that's
what he was and he's departed
forever. Peace. *Amen.*

When the priest finished he closed the book and stepped out from behind the lectern and walked toward Joe's family. The old man did not stay. Outside the sky was almost clear and the sun shined warmly on the old man, and he thought he could smell a touch of fall in the air. He walked to the car and he thought that now he had done all that he had to do and it was time for everything to end. A calm and a quiet settled on him and he was indifferent to the passing of time and he did not think about being afraid.

He was leaning against the car when Joe's family came out ten or fifteen minutes later. They walked toward the car slowly. Mr. Ross had his arm around his wife, who looked as if she had been crying, and Scott walked beside them. He was pale. Mr. Ross unlocked the door on the old man's side and reached back and unlocked the back door and held it open for his wife. He went around to the driver's side and unlocked the door and got in and unlocked the door behind him, and the old man and Scott each got in without speaking. Mr. Ross drove out of the driveway slowly. He did not speak until after he had driven for a few minutes.

"It's all going to be done late this afternoon," he said. His voice was rough and unsteady. "I've asked to have the ashes scattered."

Good the old man thought, from dust to dust. Joe would have liked that. I wonder if he knew the passage in *Hamlet* where Hamlet says that Alexander the Great's ashes might have been used to make a stopper for a beer barrel.

"Are you still coming over to the island?" the old man asked. "I've had someone fix something to eat and I've invited a few of Joe's friends to come so you could meet them."

"I don't think so," Mr. Ross said. His voice was still unsteady and he touched the corner of one eye with a finger.

"I would like to meet some of Joe's friends," Mrs. Ross said strongly. There was anger in her voice.

"I just don't think I want to do it, Jan," Mr. Ross said. He was pleading a little and all the bluster was gone. The old man listened in silence.

"Then I'll take Scott, but I'm going. Goddamn it, we refused to acknowledge anything about Joe's life when he was living, do we have to keep that up when he's dead too!" Mrs. Ross was half shouting and when she was finished she cried quietly. Scott put his hand out toward her and she slapped it away.

"Put your hand down, you damned jerk. Your brother was worth two of you and you never knew it because of that even bigger jerk in the front seat."

Scott pulled his hand back and was embarrassed, and the

old man waited for Mr. Ross to erupt. Instead, he said, "All right, I'll go," and his voice was even weaker than it had been before.

No one spoke again until they reached the motel, when the old man said that they could walk easily from the motel parking lot. Mr. Ross parked the car and shut it off. "Let's go," he said to the old man when everyone had gotten out, and they walked down the street toward the ferry, the old man and Mrs. Ross in front, Mr. Ross and Scott behind.

The ferry was already tied up when they reached the dock, and the old man paid for everyone and they went to board.

"I'm riding topside," the old man said, "but we'll be running into the wind so there'll probably be spray. You might want to ride below."

"I don't feel like getting wet," Mrs. Ross said, and she climbed aboard while a crewman watched. The men followed her.

"I think I'll ride up with Mr. Stevenson," Scott said, and Mr. and Mrs. Ross went down the steps to the inside cabin and the old man and Scott climbed to the top.

The old man took a seat at the front and Scott sat beside him. "You'll probably stay drier if you take a seat near the back," the old man said.

"That's OK. It won't be the first time I've gotten wet," Scott told him.

The old man nodded. He took off his jacket, folded it, and put it on the seat between them. The ferry was crowded and Scott looked at the young men and middle-aged men and old men around him, and all of the men looked at Scott.

The engines started, and the captain backed the boat out into the channel and then turned ahead. As he often did, the old man wondered who had abandoned the boats that now lay rotting and half-submerged in the shallows along the far bank, their hulks sadly reminiscent of times long past. The ferry's engines ran smoothly and quietly and the old man listened with pleasure to the rustle of the great reeds, now browning under the August sun, and he watched the reeds wave in the wind and he was happy to be returning to the island. Above him a few white clouds drifted in a deep blue sky and the old man thought that it was a perfect August day.

When the boat had cleared the channel the old man turned to Scott. "Your mother was pretty rough on you back there in the car," he said.

"I guess so," Scott said. "But I feel sorry for her. She's always blamed my dad for driving Joe away. I guess she thought that someday we'd all have a happy reunion, you too, and everything would be forgotten."

The old man did not answer. He watched the clamming boats. They run a conveyor along the bottom that brings up everything in its path and dumps it on another conveyor on the boat where the clams are picked out, and then the debris is dumped out the other side of the boat back into the bay.

"That's some operation," Scott said. "Those boats must take a lot of clams. I'd think that sometime there won't be any clams left."

"I don't know," the old man said, and he told Scott that Whitman had written that in the early nineteenth century lobsters were so plentiful along Long Island that farmers used them for fertilizer. As the old man spoke the boat began to go faster and spray arched up from the bow steadily and the old man felt it on his face and tasted it and was calm and waiting to join the sea.

"You were good for Joe," Scott said suddenly.

The old man turned from watching the spray.

"Joe wrote to me once in a while, you know."

The old man nodded.

"—And every time he did most of the letter was about you."

"Did you ever write back?" the old man asked. He knew the answer.

"Not very often, I guess. I wish I had."

It's too late now the old man thought, and he looked away over the water and at the rainbows made by the sunlight on the spray and something about the spray made him think of the way flying fish in the tropics burst out of the water and skim along its surface.

The island approached quickly, and the boat slowed and came to the dock in a wide circle and tied up alongside it. The old man and Scott got off first and waited for Scott's parents to come up from the cabin.

"Well, this is Cherry Grove," the old man said when they were all together. Shirtless, muscular young men in brief trunks walked about; men in Lacoste shirts meandered here and there; the sound of Gershwin's *Rhapsody in Blue* being played on an old piano came from a bar that had once been called the Island Queen but now was more dignified; two women walked closely together, talking earnestly; a brown-haired boy chased a young girl; a thin, effete man with graying hair led two yapping, nervous dogs on leashes; a group of volunteer firewomen worked with their equipment on the dock. The old man welcomed the feel of the boardwalk under his feet, and as he walked he pointed out the sights. They walked past the tiny post office; past houses trimmed with purple, houses surrounded with gaudy statuary; past a house, once elegant and now sad, that was designed to look like a miniature Rhode Island mansion; past a house with a sign that said "bottoms up." The Rosses looked at everything and Mrs. Ross watched her husband sternly.

They walked along the bay and then turned across the island toward the old man's house. It is quiet on the island because there are no cars, and as they walked they could hear the wind in the sea pines. When they came to the house the old

185

man rang the bell by the gate and then opened it and motioned for the others to precede him.

Lonny, Robert, and Mildred were sitting on the bench near the kitchen door, and they stood up and walked toward the gate. The old man introduced everyone and he smiled to see Robert wearing a sports jacket over a polo shirt, and white pants, and he squeezed Robert's hand and Robert smiled too.

Nobody knew what to say and there was an uncertain silence until Mildred asked if anyone would like coffee.

"Do you have any scotch?" Mr. Ross asked the old man.

"Certainly. Come in and I'll get it," the old man said, and they went inside. In the kitchen the old man introduced the Rosses to Carl and Elizabeth and a waiter from the restaurant.

"You must have been very proud of Joe," Elizabeth said, and Mr. Ross said softly, "We were," and then there was another silence.

"I'll get you that drink," the old man said, and he started to move toward the cupboard.

"No, I'll get it," Lonny said. "What would you like?"

"Scotch on the rocks." Mr. Ross looked at the dark part in Lonny's hair.

Lonny asked the others what they wanted to drink, and Scott asked for a beer and everyone else asked for coffee.

"Aren't you going to have a drink with me?" Mr. Ross asked the old man.

"Not this time."

"Hey, why doesn't everyone go inside, or out on the deck," Lonny said, and everyone except the waiter and Lonny moved into the front room. A tablecloth had been laid on the old man's desk, and food had been arranged on top of it. There was pâté and cold chicken slices and raw vegetables and tortellini salad and quiche and cheese and sliced ham. Part of the old man said that he would not eat, but he knew that he would be weak later when he needed strength if he did not eat

186

so he decided that sometime during the afternoon he would have a good meal.

"Well, this is all of it," the old man said. He gestured around the room.

Mrs. Ross walked over to look at the flowers. "I've always loved bird of paradise," she said.

"So have I," the old man answered. "They take a bit of the tropics with them wherever they go."

Lonny came in with drinks and he asked the old man if he was sure he didn't want anything but coffee and the old man said yes he was sure but he might have a drink later. Mr. Ross finished his scotch in two swallows.

The old man drew open the glass doors to the front deck and went out and unfolded the chairs, which were now dry, and he came back inside.

"Why doesn't everyone help themselves to something to eat," he said. "You can sit wherever you want."

Everyone but Mr. Ross and the old man took some food, and everyone stayed inside.

"Have something," the old man said to Mr. Ross.

"No thanks, but I'll take another one of these." He held his glass up.

"I'll get it," Lonny said, and he put his plate down on the corner of Joe's desk and took Mr. Ross's glass into the kitchen and brought it back full. The old man smiled at the way the women were talking in one corner and Carl and Scott and Robert were talking in another corner, and he filled a plate with food and invited Mr. Ross to come out on the deck with him. They sat in the canvas chairs and looked toward the sea.

"There are some things we have to talk about," the old man said. Mr. Ross did not answer or look at him. The old man waited for a response and when there was none he continued:

"The people here on the island have collected some

money to be used in Joe's memory. Is there anything you'd like it to go for?"

"Whatever you like," Mr. Ross said. He spoke roughly and the old man now recognized the effects of grief and part of him was sad for the man beside him but part of him was distant and indifferent.

"All right," the old man said.

"Joe had a will, you know," he went on.

Mr. Ross did not respond.

"Well," the old man said, "in it he left everything to me, but I think it should go to you if you want it."

Mr. Ross looked at the sea and the muscles in his face tightened. The old man waited for his answer.

Mr. Ross turned toward the old man. "How can God let this happen to someone in the prime of his life, someone who had so much living yet to do," he said suddenly. "Why didn't he take you? You're just an old faggot; your life is almost over."

Mr. Ross bowed his face in his hands. They had heard him inside and Scott started to come out, but the old man motioned him back and the people inside resumed a low conversation. The old man said nothing; he waited. He did not think that Mr. Ross had said everything he was going to say.

Mr. Ross looked up after a few minutes and his eyes were red and his face was wet around his eyes.

"Now I guess you'll have to recruit someone else," he said to the old man.

The old man clenched his hands and it was hard to keep silent but he did.

"Isn't that how you further your disgusting kind?" Mr. Ross said.

The old man did not let himself reply. Instead he remembered a warm September evening in New York spent with a brash, bright young man named Joe, and he also thought about the sea.

Mrs. Ross came out quickly. "I'm sure he didn't mean it," she said to the old man.

"Yes I did," Mr. Ross said. "This wouldn't have happened if Joe had never met *him*." He looked at the old man.

The old man turned away and felt tears start to rise, and then he got up and went into the house. The people from the island were standing in a group, and Scott was standing by the old man's desk looking out on the deck.

"I'm sorry," Scott said to the old man. "He's been acting very strangely since you called him about Joe."

The old man told him that it was all right he understood, and the old man thought that he really did understand and he wanted the time to pass. He put his plate with his untouched meal down on Joe's desk, and Mildred came over and put her arm around the old man and for a minute he relaxed against her shoulder and drifted.

Mrs. Ross came back inside and the old man stood up straight and Mildred stepped away.

"I think we're going to go," Mrs. Ross said. "Could you tell us how to get back to the ferry?"

"I'll walk you over," Carl told her. "I've got to be heading toward work pretty soon anyway.

"Want to come?" he asked Lonny.

"Sure," Lonny said. "I'll stop by later," he told the old man.

"I think I'm going to get some rest. Why don't you and Carl come over tomorrow morning for breakfast."

"If there's food, I'll be here," Lonny said.

"I think there's enough food in the house to feed even you for a week." The old man smiled.

Mrs. Ross and Scott said good-bye to the others and went outside to where Mr. Ross was still sitting looking at the sea. He stood up when they came out and did not look directly at the old man and did not speak. The old man led them all around the side of the house to the gate, and Scott shook his hand and Mrs. Ross kissed him on the cheek while Mr. Ross waited outside on the boardwalk.

"Listen," the old man said to Lonny and Carl, "I want to thank you for everything you've done for me in the last three days."

Mrs. Ross and Scott joined Mr. Ross outside on the walk and the old man embraced Carl and ran his hand over Lonny's hair, and the old man knew that this was the important good-bye but that he could not let them know it.

"No sweat," Lonny said. "We'll be here to help you eat some of the food in the morning too."

The old man smiled and he touched Lonny's hair again and then rested his hand on Lonny's shoulder, and he realized how much he had come to like Lonny in the few days he had known him and he thought that he would miss him and then he thought that there would be no missing where he was going, and then he turned and said good-bye to Joe's family while Mr. Ross looked away, and the old man said good-bye to Lonny and Carl again and he closed the gate behind them. As soon as the gate was closed Lonny rang the bell and the old man smiled at him and smiled to hear the sound of the bell, and he walked to the house, eager for the time to pass.

Inside, the waiter and Robert and Elizabeth were putting away food and cleaning while Mildred directed from a chair.

"How was it?" Mildred asked, and the old man said that the funeral had been simple and very brief, and he said that he was tired. He seemed distant and unreachable.

"Are you OK?" Elizabeth asked.

"I'm fine," the old man said, "just tired."

"Oh, I'd like you to decide what to do with the money," he said to Robert, and he thanked Elizabeth and Mildred for the money they had given.

"Are you sure?" Robert asked.

The old man said yes and again he said that he was tired,

190

and when the kitchen was clean everyone prepared to leave. The old man thanked the waiter and gave him some money, and he left first.

"Do you want us to come over tomorrow?" Mildred asked.

"You can help Lonny eat all this food, if you want," the old man said. He knew that by the next evening there would be people at his house and he was glad that there would be food for them.

"We'll be here," Elizabeth said.

Everyone walked outside, and the old man thanked them by the gate and he hugged Robert good-bye and kissed his cheek and he kissed Elizabeth and Mildred.

"Remember, we all love you," Mildred told him.

"I know," the old man said very quietly and he opened the gate and everyone left. He stood watching them until they turned down a boardwalk toward the bay, and then he closed the gate and went back inside.

The old man fixed himself a plate of food and ate it and washed his plate and fork and put them away, and then he went carefully through the house, examining things as if he had never seen them before. He noted the way the toothbrush holder was fastened to the bathroom wall; he touched the stove and turned on a burner until it glowed, then turned it off; he went into the room under the loft and looked at the books and ran his hands along their spines and part of him regretted that he would never know everything in them; he went to his desk and examined the pen he wrote with and then got the unopened letter to Joe from Joe's desk and sat and wrote a short note and put the note and the letter into a larger envelope and put two stamps on it and left it on his desk, and then he went out onto the deck and stood with both hands on the rail, facing the sea.

I must not be afraid he thought, there is nothing to fear. At the end I will be very tired and it will be over quickly; three

191

or four minutes without oxygen and then I'll be unconscious and I won't care. I've always loved the sea. I wish it could be a tropical sea now but it's not and this will do as well the old man thought, and as he tried to make himself calm he knew that he was afraid.

Someone waved from the beach and the old man waved back and went inside and climbed up to the loft to look at the clock. It was almost five and he decided to take a nap. He looked out over the room below and saw the bird of paradise flowers and went down to get them. He took the flowers out of the water and took them into the bathroom and dried their stems and then took them back up to the loft and laid them on the bed. He undressed and lay on his side beside the flowers and looked into them. He thought of the tropics and remembered walking around the island of Bora Bora with Joe and looking at the changing, savage faces of the mountain Otematu that stands sharply against the sky and he remembered swimming in the lagoon and looking down through the water at the white sand and he passed into a quiet sleep and dreamed of turquoise seas and sweet tropical breezes.

When the old man awoke it was dark and he looked at the clock and saw that it was almost ten and he was pleased that he had slept so long. Above him the stars shined brightly and through the side windows he could see a thin crescent of moon and he tried to be calm and he felt a little distant from himself. He stroked the blue tongue of one of the flowers and then got up slowly, leaving the flowers on the bed.

The old man dressed carefully and climbed down from the loft. He looked around the room with sadness and he picked up the pile of bills from Joe's desk and he picked up the note to Joe's friend from his desk and went outside. As he stepped onto the walk he rang the bell by the gate.

He was afraid of the sea now and he knew that he was and he decided that he would like just one more time to see a friend, not to say good-bye but just to be with someone for a few minutes to give himself courage. He walked toward Carl's house first and as he walked he touched the pines lining the walk, enjoying the feel of the sharp needles against his hand, and he carefully picked and crushed and smelled some bayberry leaves as if he had never done it before, and when he reached Carl's house he saw that there were no lights burning and he turned back and then turned down the walk that led past Robert's house, and when he saw that Robert's house was also dark his fear grew and he continued on slowly toward the bay and then turned toward the post office. He posted the letters he was carrying and then walked slowly through the town. He heard the pulsing of music from one disco as he passed and the sound of the people inside tempted him but he did not stop, and then he passed the restaurant where Robert and Carl worked and he looked through the open door into that disco but although he walked very slowly no one noticed him and he continued on toward the sea, trying not to be afraid and trying not to cry.

At the bottom of the steps over the dunes the old man removed his shoes and socks and rolled up his pants legs and put his socks into his shoes and carried them both as he walked out into the water. He was glad that the night was not too cool and as he walked in the shallow water toward the east he shuddered at the gentle wash of the waves over his feet and although he tried not to think but just exist he was crushed with dread and fear. When he was well past the last house in the Grove but still some distance away from the first house in the Pines he walked up on the beach and took off his clothes and piled them neatly on his shoes above the high-tide line and he ran his hands over his body and thought that it was not too bad for an old man and then he went down to the water again and walked out into it until it was almost up to his knees. He was very afraid now and he shivered at the chill of the water and he bent down and picked up some of the water with his hands and wet his face and arms and thighs and chest and then he walked out a few more feet and dove carefully through the surf and when he came up he swam away from the shore with slow, measured, steady strokes, saving his strength for the distance to come, and as he swam he allowed his mind to drift and he thought about Elizabeth and Mildred, whose love for each other was strong and proud and unchanging, and he thought about Carl and Lonny, who were so young and vital, and he missed them all and when he thought about missing them he thought that he would like to take a farewell look at the island he had loved for so many years, not only for his friends there and for the unselfconscious lifestyle it allowed but also for its natural beauty. No, he told himself, you cannot look back you must go on, and he continued to swim toward the dark line where the sea rose up to meet the starry sky and as he swam he remembered recurring summer days of blazing suns and azure skies that faded into crystalline nights aglow with starlight, those days when the sand seemed to dance in the heat and those clear and moonless nights when the beach was softly illuminated by starlight when he would walk with Joe to the dunes by the forest, far from any artificial lights, and sit and look at the stars, so clear and so bright they could be touched, at least in the imagination. The old man did not intend to stop, but as he thought about the stars he found himself treading water and not moving forward and he turned then and swam a little back in the direction of the shore using his arms to push his head and chest up out of the water so he could see over the waves and as he looked toward the beach he thought he saw lights come on in Carl's house but he was not certain because he was moving up and down with the waves and with his strokes and he swam a little more toward shore until he knew that he could see the lights in Carl's house and then he was overpowered with great, irresistible waves of emotion and he started to weep and his breath came harder and the waves of emotion grew until he sobbed uncontrollably into the sea and as he sobbed and gasped he swallowed some

194

seawater, and suddenly he was terrified. He swam for the shore as hard as he could then, gasping and sobbing, and laughing through his tears that he still lived, but he had come a long way out and the current was hard and strong and the old man began to tire when there was still a long way to go and he began to think that he might not make it and he tried to stifle his sobs to save his energy for the swim but he could not, and when he could not control his breathing he knew that he was going to die and he wanted his last thoughts to be about Joe and he forced himself to think of Joe's voice and his soft long hair and his warm smooth skin browned by the sun and the curves of muscle in his chest and legs and arms and as he thought about Joe his breathing gradually became more regular, and although he still wept he began to feel Joe's presence and he shut his eyes and swam stroke for stroke with the beautiful young man who swam beside him and whom he had loved so much and the young man began to increase the pace and the old man swam still harder and his arms and legs began to feel warm and comfortable and the strokes began to require less effort and soon the old man's tears stopped and he could feel Joe saying come on Old Man we will do this together and he swam in a place without time, and then in the distance he heard a roar and he knew that he was drifting into unconsciousness and he did not fight it but allowed himself to slip down into the water and the feeling of warmth in his arms and legs spread throughout his body and he was calm and then in his last moments of consciousness he again thought of Joe and first he thought I am too tired but then he swam beside the young man once more and pulled his way to the surface and when he again heard a roar he opened his eyes and in front of him he could see the waves swelling and cresting before they fell onto the shore and then a wave broke over him and pushed him down into the water and as he fought the surf he felt the sand under his feet and when he stood up he was only a few yards from the beach, and again the old man wept.

195